Chloe Leiberman
(Sometimes Wong)

Chloe Leiberman

(Sometimes Wong)

A novel by

Carrie Rosten

Delacorte Press

Published by
Delacorte Press
an imprint of
Random House Children's Books
a division of Random House, Inc.
New York

The trademark Delacorte Press is registered in the U.S. Patent and Trademark Office
and in other countries.

Visit us on the Web! www.randomhouse.com/teens
Educators and librarians, for a variety of teaching tools, visit us at
www.randomhouse.com/teachers

Library of Congress Cataloging-in-Publication Data
Rosten, Carrie.
Chloe Leiberman (sometimes Wong) / Carrie Rosten.
p. cm.
Summary: Chloe, an aspiring fashion designer, dreams of going to design school in
London, but first has to tell her parents that she does not plan to go to college.
ISBN 0-385-73247-3 (trade) — ISBN 0-385-90271-9 (glb)
[1. High schools—Fiction. 2. Schools—Fiction. 3. Jews—California—Fiction.
4. Chinese Americans—Fiction. 5. Racially mixed peoples—Fiction.
6. California—Fiction.] I. Title.
PZ7.R7234Ch 2005
[Fic]—dc22
2004028995

The text of this book is set in 12.5-point Apollo MT.

Book design by Angela Carlino

Printed in the United States of America

September 2005

10 9 8 7 6 5 4 3 2 1

BVG

For Alex

The underlying notion of fashion is of "making," "forming," or "shaping."

—John Ayto, *Dictionary of Word Origins*

It was like this. Chloe Leiberman (sometimes Wong) might have been a senior without a plan but she was a girl with a dream (which matters much more anyhow since plans can be overrated). So, Chloe finally sent this, what you're about to read, to design school. It's like an application but not. It's a little long and strange and unconventional but so, as you shall see, is Chloe.

part one

Personal Data/Family

[Where does a girl *even* begin?]

Wong-Leiberman 101

DO: Opt for pearls on special occasions to please your mother

DON'T: Think wearing pearls will get you off the opting-out-of-college hook

So Chloe Wong-Leiberman was a senior without a plan. She was also a Chinese Jewish WASP with a fashion disorder. What, you ask, is a fashion disorder? It's not what you might be thinking—like, someone with zero sense of style and no fashion sense whatsoever. Au contraire, Chloe had plenty of style and tons of fashion sense. Too much. She'd even say she's obsessed.

And do you know what obsession is like? To eat, drink, think, breathe, dream, and be totally and hopelessly consumed by something? This, as you might already know, kinda sucks.

Chloe was totally and hopelessly *obsessed* with everything related to clothing, shoes, and accessories—and not just her own. She was obsessed with *your* clothing, shoes, and accessories too—so obsessed that eventually she had to diagnose herself with, well, her fashion disorder. (We'll cover the symptoms shortly.) For right now just know that this FD thing, as she liked to call it, was extremely problematic. Especially because her FD was the reason she was on the verge of her high school graduation without a postgrad plan. And to be a senior without a postgrad plan in the Wong-Leiberman household was a gigantic DON'T.

You know, like there are DOs and DON'Ts in fashion, well, there are DOs and DON'Ts for Wong-Leibermans too. Like, DO plan on applying to, getting into, and then attending a REALLY HARD college. Like, DON'T even think about NOT applying to, getting rejected from, and *not* attending a really hard college. And well, Chloe had about the same chance to get into a REALLY HARD college that Melissa Rivers had to, like, cut the cord and get off that red carpet.

In a perfect world (and you know we don't live in one of those) Chloe wouldn't even apply to college at all; she'd apply to fashion school, Central Saint Martins in London to be exact. But it was in London and it was an art school and art schools didn't count as really hard colleges, don't you know? And even though the fam had lowered the traditional A-list bar out of sheer necessity, Saint Martins was definitely *not* on-the-list. Not even the B list. Or C list. It was on the don't-even-think-about-applying list. Not that she was going to since that would require some confidence and Chloe didn't have much of that.

And despite her seriously diverse background like . . . Asian shame, Jewish guilt, and some good old-fashioned WASP contempt, Chloe Wong-Leiberman didn't chant or go to temple and she had never even been to church (although she had been in a church parking lot one time to buy these insane Bakelite bangles at some dead lady's estate sale). Prime opps to score vintage. Chloe just loved vintage. Wells Park, where she lived, was low on vintage. That's because everything there was new, new, new!

Wells Park was this ritzy "gated community" nestled by the sea with three country clubs and, like, two Chinese people. One of those Chinese people was her mom, Lucinda, and the other was her grandma who had just moved in, Pau-Pau. (That means Grandma in Cantonese and Cantonese is one of a zillion dialects spoken by Chinese people.) If Chloe were to include her sixteen-year-old brother, Mitchell, and herself then that actually would make it *three whole* Chinese people. Definitely a Wells Park record.

Wells Park was Southern Cali *all the way*. It was all about pampas grass and palm trees and Pilates bodies (aspiring at least)—continually drenched in sun and skin, lots of terry cloth and flip-flops and patrolled by, like, fake policemen.

The Wong-Leibermans lived in a three-story Mc-Mansion; you know, one of those humungous homes that all look the same. This one was custom built eighteen years earlier by Lucinda to mimic an early-American colonial style, complete with green plantation shutters and a red-shingled roof and financed by none other than the Bacon Bringer himself, Chloe's dad, Stanley.

Stanley was senior partner at the Newport firm Schmukla, Schitty, and Schizer—a midsize law firm specializing in mergers and acquisitions. That meant he made a considerable chunk of change doling out tax advice to rich people who "sheltered" cash on faraway islands with names like Parakeet Bay and Gold Mountain. He did all the native Wells Park locals' taxes and that's why the Leibermans were the first part-Jewish family to be sponsored at the Shore, the first country club to arrive on the Wells Park scene some forty years ago (which is way old for Wells Park).

Stan, hands down, was a workaholic. Mitchell, Mr. All-Star-Everything, was a dutiful workaholic in training who liked to gloat and flex and praise the Market or Republicans or Himself and not necessarily in that order. Chlo's Chinese grandma (again that would be Pau-Pau, pronounced Paw-Paw, not Po-Po or Poo-Poo), well, she only moved in a month ago to recover from surgery—a major stomach cancer operation that removed, like, her entire esophagus. Then there was

Zeyde. That's Yiddish for Grandpa. Zeyde rhymes with lady. You don't know what Yiddish is? Check out the glossary in the back for my definition.

Zeyde wasn't official at 450 Avocado Lane but he liked to pop by from time to time to nosh or nap or lament the fact that his grandkids were never bar mitzvahed. Then there was Wally, Lucinda's beloved fifty-pound Corgi. Seriously—the dog weighed fifty pounds. That's, like, twice what he was supposed to weigh. At this rate he was going down fast.

Tonight was Chinese New Year, which was always a stressful affair, so Lucinda was especially worked up over the holiday menu. Zeyde was coming in from La Jolla and he and Pau had way different dietary needs. He was a kosher diabetic allergic to wheat, no matzoh for him, and she had major digestive issues particularly of the lactose kind, no Brie or gelato for her. Have you ever experienced the gas that comes out of a lactose-intolerant grandma? It's VERY unfortunate.

Lucinda couldn't be bothered to cook anyhow (an oxymoron right there for a Chinese mom), or, according to Chloe, the only way her mother could stick to suffering on her latest diet.

Chloe hoped to tell the parentals about her opting-out-of-college situation that night, one at a time, preferably in the company of a housekeeper or grandparent—always good, strategic buffers. Or if things got out of hand she always could use Wally. He made a highly padded shield.

Since Mitchell would be home soon with the nightly "Mitchell Report" to recap all of his latest coups on and off the Eden Prep playing field and Stanley would be slipping through the side door any second looking ready to apologize for something whether he did it or not (he probably didn't), Chloe had little time to break the big news to the toughest nut, her mom—sans Chinese New Year novelty sweater, of course. Oh, yes, every Chinese New Year Lucinda enjoyed purchasing select family members a festive big-buttoned cardigan number, all Mr. Rogers style, in sickening candy apple red. To be SANS festive novelty sweater on the Chinese New Year was a big ol' DON'T, but only if you were Stan or Chloe since rules didn't seem to apply to Mitch.

Chloe, mind you, would rather be naked—or dead—or both—before she would ever ever wear this Chinese New Year novelty sweater thing—to bed even! After Chloe had "lost" hers for the past twelve years Lucinda finally gave up this season but the Battle of the Novelty Sweater was a Pyrrhic victory at best, hard fought but not quite won and sorely remembered to this day.

Last year Chloe had tried to compromise. For real. That's why she decided to alter hers, just a tad, by dying the cardigan fuchsia—something not all too well received. To try to defend herself was moot. Chloe had done something unthinkable: She had vandalized both the sweater and the claw-foot tub, now dyed an irreversible shade of Betsey Johnson pink. (And, FYI, the

Wong-Leiberman household was pastel all the way, so loud and bright a la Betsey was a big ol' DON'T.) Since it *was* Chinese New Year her mother stood dressed for the festive occasion which was exactly why Chloe never made it past the service stairs into enemy territory at all! She was paralyzed by the potential sight—a sweeping migraine took shape—and then, something unavoidable occurred—something that happened whenever she was about to bear witness to bad fashion. Especially on her mother.

FULL-on Red Carpetosis! It was the most common symptom of her FD. In seconds, Chloe was whisked away onto her own little red carpet where she, alone, stood under lights and cameras and just HAD TO discuss slash critique her mother's latest. But, like, she was the only one on this red carpet, sans hair or makeup, and the segment never aired anywhere except in her head. She even had a one-sheet with notes and everything. It looked like this:

THE CARPETOSIS DIAGNOSIS
SUBJECT: Lucinda Wong-Leiberman, aka Mom
FAMILY HISTORY: N/A yet
STYLE SYMPTOMS: color-phobic yet does pastels (one at a time), loves loafers, hates open-toe anything, matches everything—usually stemware to scoop-neck cardigans, never ever mixes labels, enjoys satin headbands and shapeless shifts in tiny floral patterns. Channels Martha Stewart (preindictment, of course), LOTS.

Chloe reviewed her imagined notes, the carpet was ablaze with glaring lights, and she was ready to go.

And-we're-live-from—

"Oh hi, me, it's me, live from the Red Carpet with today's Carpetosis Diagnosis, here to break it down for Lucinda Wong-Leiberman on the most auspicious day of the year, the first day of the Chinese New Year, this the Year of the Tiger. So we know by now Lucinda plays it safe with one of three unfortunate, sucky looks. Sucky look number one, we'll just call 'Aspiring Pilates Mom' (relaxed-fit khakis, three-quarter-sleeve polos, sensible shoes). This look sadly shows Lucinda will go to any lengths to try to blend in with every other identically outfitted Wells Park mom even though that's impossible (a) because she's Chinese and (b) she's maybe used her House of Yogilates membership, like, two times.

"Sucky Look Number two we'll just call 'Aspiring Corporate Mom' (early nineties, charcoal gray, get-out-of-my-way-I'm-late Armani suit). This is, like, some futile attempt for Lucinda to channel the high-powered world of finance she never experienced let alone conquered so she always ends up looking kinda tragic. I mean, she *is* a housewife in the burbs, not some I banker on Wall Street.

"Wanna know why? Cuz it was like this. Nineteen years ago, just weeks after being recruited by Sanderson Consulting in New York, Lucinda met Stan. She was ready to board her Kennedy-bound flight at SFO, matching Tumi bags set to go, but then Stanley literally bumped into her and an unlikely magic transpired over a spilled cup of instant coffee on an Ann Taylor button-down. She never did make that flight and quit the profession before she ever even began, opting instead to become Stan's full-on wife, and shortly after, a not-so-full-on mom. Which brings us to . . .

"Sucky Look Number Three, 'Aspiring Connecticut Homemaker!' (oversized fisherman's sweater, matching jodhpurs, L.L. Bean wellies). This, no doubt, is the look that's by far Lucinda's fave. Dressed up like this she's the VISION of Greenwich itself, and in, like, total Ralph Lauren, she probably pretends to host these very exclusive weekly salons in her lovingly restored nineteenth-century REAL colonial, musing by a perpetual fire that, like, mirrors the amber hues of September leaves tumbling forth from ancient, stately trees—strolling hand in hand with her erudite, philanthropic-type husband who's, like, maybe an expert in Greek—someone who'll clasp her woolen mittened hand tight as they, say, savor the air of a crisp and true New England fall. . . .

"But hold on. This fantasy is *by far* the farthest from the truth which is why it disturbs me the MOST. She might be a WASP mind trapped in a Chinese body but Lucinda has never even been to Connecticut! Wells Park is all about new money on the West Coast anyhow where the temperature rarely dives below seventy so no one's about to bust out with wool or wellie anything unless it's Zeyde playing Santa at Christmas. He's a Christmas-tree Jew. Kinda hypocritical, wouldn't you agree?"

The lights dimmed, the Red Carpet rolled up and POOF! disappeared.

Chloe wanted to empathize with her mom at least a teensy bit. Her mom's conflicted fashion statements were, after all, like, therapy. They were important role-playing games where Lucinda could at least try on identities even if they weren't for real.

Tonight, . . . Lucinda was featuring some *very* all-black situation (a clear sign she needed to be taken seriously). It was kinda festive, kinda fancy, and kinda corporate—definitely high collared *with* shoulder pads. Yuh-huhhh. Festive, fancy, corporate, and hold on . . . ethnic too?

Whoa . . . Definitely a bold departure from seasons past. Lucinda was dressed like some kind of imperial Chinese matador, metallic slotted spoon held at attention. Her dramatic bolero jacket was shiny and square—a blinding jacquard print with bell sleeves paired with what appeared to be (oh god why) very pleated (hmm) wide-leg pants. The pants ballooned over two-toned black and tan ballet flats (typical), exposing some (ew) opaque and (double-ew) nude panty hose.

Well, OK. Chlo knew this certainly wasn't the worst thing her mother had ever worn but it wasn't making any top-ten list either (not that she was making a list). The bolero jacket was especially displeasing since it featured these jumbo pearl buttons, champagne colored, each the size of golf balls. They even had dangling gold tassels. Lucinda's bobbed hair was tucked behind her ears with her requisite mono-grammed satin headband, tiny seed pearls outlining her preferred initials, LL. Oyy vey. EW.

And then, just as Chloe tried to move forward she was struck. She felt clammy, dizzy, faint . . . and *Oh god, not here, not now.* It was too late. She had seen enough and was going to hallucinate.

The stairs closed up all around her and began to spin out of control. A fuchsia curtain wiped away Lucinda's silhouette, the kitchen slowly faded from view, and POOF! Chloe was no-longer-there-at-all. Everything in the kitchen, like, disappeared.

Chloe stood all alone once again in a tiny little studio, far, far away . . . preparing for—*Wheel of Fashion.* Kinda. Complete with audience participation and, like, a grinning Botoxed lady spinning the wheel. Together, Chloe and the wheel *had* to determine the fate of the fashion victim at hand, Lucinda Wong-Leiberman, and fix every single last faux pas. At least they'd try!

DING DING DING! The wheel stopped and Lucinda now stood transformed. She featured a sleeveless cowl-neck blouse in cream silk paired over dark denim jeans—straight leg, no pleats, natural waist, falling midheel over a pair of tweed slingbacks, two, maybe, three inches. Nothing hookerish but still kinda hot. Mom hot, of course (if there is such a thing). Headband be gone! Instead, Lucinda's bobbed and banged hair was straightened and slick, pulled completely back in a neat chignon sans bow or bell. Smallish gold and diamond hoops replaced the mammoth pearl studs, a threaded gold cuff encircled an elbow, and the woman now stood relaxed and at ease instead of like a frozen Popsicle about to melt. For one glorious minute, at least in her head, Chloe's mother actually had style.

But, you see, this was just a hallucination—a fantasy—a mirage! And all hallucinations, good or bad, must come to an end. It wasn't like Chloe consciously chose to hallucinate about re-dressing people! It was just something that automatically kicked in, like, to try to alleviate stress, kinda like serotonin but not. Or is that endorphins that do that stress-relieving thing?

Lucinda didn't even notice that Chloe was standing at the entrance to her Shabby Chic slash Williams-Sonoma shrine at all. Why? Because she was very pre-occupied studying the low-carb, wheat-free matzoh ball soup, that's why. All helpless, she waved her ladle up and down like some petulant child left to swim in the pool for the first time without floaties. Beneath her, the lone matzoh clump looked like something that had died a long time ago and wasn't too into being resuscitated.

"But Lupe said just add water and stir!" Lucinda threw her skinny arms up in the air and pleaded for sympathy. Pau naturally ignored her. She was dozing off in the light-soaked breakfast nook while half engaged in what apparently was a favorite pastime, solitaire. Her signature blue slippers dangled from the chintz-upholstered bench a good six inches off the floor.

Lucinda started tapping a silver spoon against the

bubbling pot, once, twice, then like an outright gong. Pau slammed down her pudgy fists and a queen of hearts went flying into the soup.

"Hi-yaaah! Kok nay gan tuh!" Pau snorted. She shuffled toward the Viking range and kicked Wally aside (not, like, hard or anything). Lucinda gasped while Pau began to stir and smooth the mealy pot, grumbling the whole time in mixed-up Cantonese. Chloe managed to make out something that sounded like mother white ghost cook, or lousy ghost soup, or something like that. In typical fashion, her mother and grandmother started slinging bilingual insults and wheatless matzoh, but then, her mom abruptly stopped—finally noticing her daughter.

"*Don't* tell me *that's* what you plan to wear to *my* dinner tonight, Chloe Wong?"

"What's wrong with it?" Chloe asked. She had worn pearls and everything.

Her mother grimaced. "You reject my novelty sweaters and yet an 'Ole!' T-shirt is not exactly fancy, now is it?" Lucinda really overemphasized the word "fancy," which she knew was, like, Chloe's least favorite adjective, ever.

"It's really a 'Go Lakers!' T but some of the letters are faded. Plus no one said we were doing tea at the Ritz."

Chloe tried scooping up Wally for support but he wouldn't budge. Poor Wally: fat, dumb, and lookin' for love in all the wrong places.

"—And I don't bill four hundred an hour so my

daughter can look like she pulled clothes outta a trash can!" Oy gevalt. Stan was home. This prompted Wally to start humping a barstool. (Like I said, he looked for love in all the wrong places.) For real, if only Stanley spent more QT with Wally then maybe the dog wouldn't have to hump or eat everything all the time and oh god now he was simultaneously humping *and* trying to eat Stan's way-too-long headset cord—a cord-ploy Stan deliberately tangled himself up in to avoid conversation. It was crafty . . . but, like, necessary protection too.

"But, Daddy, you gave me this T-shirt!" Chloe couldn't believe her bad timing or for that matter that she'd just called Stan "Daddy."

"When you were five!" he hollered. "Which, I might add, was when I worked for peanuts at the DA and your mother and I couldn't afford to buy you new clothes." Her dad should talk! He was currently in his fave uniform of baggy cargo shorts and a beat-up Hawaiian shirt that looked like a pack of Crayolas threw up all over it. The man might have been color-blind but he definitely was *not* color-phobic.

"See, Chloe. Naturally, your father agrees. Go change."

"But I don't want to!" Chloe cried, feeling all of five.

"Why must you make everything so complicated? You know good and well that holidays are dress-up days! Easy. Simple. A dress perhaps?" Chloe's mother shot Stan a fierce, please-concur-now look.

Stan sensed confrontation. He hated confrontation.

"Chloe Wong, in half an hour I expect to see you at my table changed into something fancy *and* appropriate," Lucinda continued.

"But this *is* my interpretation of 'fancy' and 'appropriate.' "

Lucinda cornered Chloe, ladle pointed like a spear.

"DO-NOT-PROVOKE-ME-CHLOE-WONG! I AM UNDER A GREAT DEAL OF PRESSSSURE ALREADYY!" Turning red as a beet, she jabbed the ladle in Chloe's direction, inching dangerously close.

"Hui, Lucindaw!" Pau-Pau interjected. "Let the girl be."

She planted herself firmly between them, slurping loud on a piece of gingerroot.

"Chloee-girl changed already. No need make change one more time." Pau-Pau shuffled out of the kitchen, farting as she did. Way to go, Pau, Chloe thought. At least there was one ally in the room. And even if she did communicate in bodily noises better than English Chloe felt momentarily vindicated all the same. Holding her nose, she remembered why dairy was such a DON'T.

The kitchen was totally polluted.

Spring and Secrets

DO: Wear protective head covering when about to drop a bomb

DON'T: Pretend like aforementioned protective head covering is a yoosual accessory

Spring lowered her lemon beanie over her golden, freckled face, for shaaame. No wonder she wore a beanie! She'd just gone public with some scandalous information and needed a place to hide.

Spring Beckett had been their longtime neighbor, friend, and up until Chloe "transferred" out of elitist Eden Prep two years ago, carpool companion since she and Chloe were five.

But Spring had officially defected to the Right—the other side, the DARK side—the Mitchell side. She was lost and gone forever. Chloe felt as if her entire closet had been raided and ransacked and resold by some sheisty traitor.

"Relax, Chlo, we haven't really done anything." Spring opened her bright blue eyes wide, feigning innocence.

"Rela— This is statutory . . . statutory something. Spring, it's like incest!"

Not to mention the highest form of treason!

Once upon a time Chloe and Mitchell weren't at war but that changed once they were sentenced to Eden Prep and Mitchell became this whole new fake person. The uniform, like, brainwashed him or something.

Oh, and, the infamous Bow-Tie incident severed their ties completely. Just know for now that it involved a huge fiasco in a Brooks Brothers dressing room.

Chloe flung off a stack of mismatched Lucite bangles and switched them for a single leather cuff instead—a really tight one.

"Chloe, Mitch is sixteen and I'm seventeen so really, it can't be statutory anything."

"Spring, how can you possibly think this is kosher? You've known Mitchell since he wore, like, bumblebee Velcro shoes and green OshKosh overalls!"

"Isn't kosher? This coming from Hi-my-boyfriend-like-graduated-from-high-school-before-we-were-even-born!"

Chloe threw a sequined pillow at her harping friend. Her soon to be ex-friend at this rate.

"I'm not *even* going to dignify that with a response."

Turning away, she went to the window to light what she promised herself would be her *last cigarette ever*. Outside row after row of identical manicured lawns glistened, the requisite stamp of a stately Wells Park McMansion.

"I thought you quit," Spring whispered, highly concerned. Chloe took a long and pensive drag and ashed carelessly into her mother's pink and peach rosebushes below. Chloe totally rued the day her boyfriend Dante ever gave her that first, ill-fated Marlboro Red. Smoke was horrendous for her clothes. She had a rule that she'd only smoke in her smoking sweatshirt, which was exactly what she had on right now.

Chloe sighed. "I did quit. But that was yesterday."

"But what about today?" Spring asked, her long blond ponytail bouncing to the side.

"Today I unquit, Spring." Chloe squinted at Spring's tank top and reached to adjust the lopsided spaghetti strap back over her bra.

"DON'T reveal bra strap unless bra strap is cute, which today it's not."

Chloe couldn't help but blurt this out loud. It didn't look right and when things didn't look right she just had to say something.

"Sorry, Spring. You know how my FD situation gets when I'm stressed out."

They laughed awkwardly. But it wasn't funny. It *was* for real. Wanna know how this "FD" all came about?

★ ★ ★

CHLOE'S CONDITION: What is a fashion disorder?

So Chlo had loved any and all things related to clothing, shopping, designing, and accessorizing since forever. She used to escape into her grandma's closet in a diaper and booties and crawl back out featuring *full-on wardrobe*—scarves tied as makeshift dresses, tangled in a web of crazy beads, eventually teetering around in slides and heels. She ate, breathed, and apparently even breast-fed in separates, shoes, and accessories. Everything always had to go together but nothing could be too matchy-matchy. Accessories had to be angled just so and she'd die if she ever saw anyone else wearing the same shoes she was.

Her closet had a rotating theme each season and was, like, a color-coded shrine. All her vintage Ts were rolled up perfectly, color coordinated, and *arranged* by graphic. For instance, her first grouping was Americana so there were sixteen ringers and a bunch of Ts with faded iron-ons of, like, the Dukes of Hazzard, trucks, pigs with little bows . . . that kind of thing. All her blue jeans were hanging on a solo rack—a wave of dark indigo turning into the palest shade of Pacific blue. Colored cords hung directly opposite white cargos—a crisp wave of buttercream fading into paper white. (Kinda like a Pantone chart but not.) Tops were, like, totally hard to negotiate in a single closet (even if it was a floor-through walk-in), so we won't go there since that would take up too much space. Just realize the system was *down*. *Everything* had its right place.

Dressing herself well was—well, really the only thing Chloe Wong-Leiberman felt she did right! But then, come seventh grade, she wasn't allowed to do it at all. At least, from seven to three when she was forced to wear a uniform at Eden Prep—a really bad one too.

One day after failing a pop quiz in prealgebra she went outside to get some fresh air (which Eden Prep did have lots of). A sea of loafers after polos after loafers after polos was passing her by when, suddenly, POOF! the uniforms all transformed! In a flash, a select few students featured looks she had totally created and approved! It was like some switch automatically flicked on inside and released something really powerful— again, kinda like serotonin but not.

By eighth grade this curious phenomenon occurred outside school too. She could be shopping at the Promenade and boom—change the entire third floor from frumpy to fabulous in, like, two seconds flat.

Initially, Chloe found this very amusing, a helpful way not to have to look at what was in front of her. Then she realized she couldn't make it stop. It was happening everywhere, every time she set her almond-shaped eyes on any unfortunately dressed person. Plus, she found herself offering commentary—most of the time to herself, but sometimes ALOUD. Kinda like Tourette's.

That was it. To be obsessed with her own clothing was one thing, to be obsessed with yours was another, to spontaneously hallucinate wasn't exactly normal but at least it was something she could easily hide from other people, but, like, to run the risk of commenting on what someone was wearing with something random—even mean—ALOUD! Now this was unacceptable. A big ol' horrifying DON'T.

Chloe was determined to find out what was wrong with her. She concluded she must have a "condition." So she diagnosed it herself—well, with tentative help from Spring too, way back when she still went to Eden Prep and they were BFF, for real.

It was a picture-perfect Southern California day and Chlo was wearing these vintage OP board shorts with horizontal orange and gray stripes with a perfectly worn-in Eden Prep T. It was after gym but before lunch and she and Spring were in that Monday morning third-period netherworld called "health"—that dubious elective eighth graders eagerly anticipated in order to nap, slack off, smoke pot, or write text messages to crushes they never intended to send. Mr. Materian was their narcoleptic health teacher, a well-meaning thirtysomething who prided himself on enlightening the Eden Prep elite about the big, bad world of VD, the merits of condom usage, and the perils of intravenous drug use. Of these no-duh matters, Chloe already knew plenty.

The *only* area that really piqued her interest was mental illness and the possibility she might have one—a disease, a disorder, a "something" that could finally explain why for so many years she had been the way she was. She knew there had to be an answer in that bible of mental illness, the DSM-IV, *The Diagnostic and Statistical Manual of Mental Disorders.* This red leather–bound volume glowed before Chloe's eyes like a sacred tome of the Illuminati. She needed that book. She wanted it right then and there. She announced this to Spring, who being the dutiful friend and strategic klepto she was, snuck up on Mr. Materian during his narcoleptic daze and swiped the text. But after several arduous and frustrating hours the two burgeoning diagnosticians discovered that the right terminology didn't quite exist. No single disorder perfectly described Chloe's ills—yet. So, mavericks that they were, the girls decided to coin a new phrase, thus labeling Chloe's condition a "fashion disorder."

They marked the occasion by returning "the Book" to Mr. Materian wrapped in a "festive" pink and blue bow—gigantic F and D eloquently penned over what would be his dubious new book jacket. Chloe would forever feel indebted and connected to Spring for sharing that life-shaping diagnosis.

Here are the symptoms in full. There are shades of OCD, ADD, Tourette's, and yes, even dissociative identity disorder.

Symptom #1: obsessive thoughts

Chloe's *clearly* obsessed. She is, however, still able to function in the world without her friends and family ever really knowing the extent of her full-fledged obsession.

Symptom #2: compulsive behavior
Chloe is compelled to shop, sew, or sometimes even style passersby. There are of course the requisite spontaneous shopping sprees, the items she just can't live without, and she'll never be able to pass up a dollar fabric bin without scavenging through the whole thing. She's also a sucker for online shopping. Chloe costume-changes several times a day to best fit her ever-changing moods, then takes a picture of the look with her vintage Polaroid. She labels all accompanying photos with pink Sharpies and sometimes makes a collage.

Symptom #3: vocal tics
OK, so this is that sorta-Tourette's thing. Chloe doesn't blurt obscenities or bark aloud or anything like that but she will blurt nonsequitur comments in the middle of class like "Love your belt" or when making out with her boyfriend Dante she might say, "Lame socks!" Most of the time she keeps this commentary to herself but occasionally something will slip out and she'll have to apologize or pretend like she said nothing at all.

Symptom #4: hallucinations
We've covered this one, right? Well, imagine having a pair of built-in glasses that trans-formed everyone around you. This is what it

was like for Chloe. Now imagine not being able to take those glasses off, like, ever.

Symptom #5: impulsivity
See symptom number two.

Symptom #6: distractability
See symptoms number one and two. Oh, and four and seven.

Symptom #7: Red Carpetosis
We also covered this one already. This symptom is probably the most severe since it's been getting in the way of things she was supposed to have been doing like, oh, taking her SATs, going to PE (not that you should have to go to PE), applying to colleges, and stuff like that.

As you can see, Chlo's FD was a peculiar hybrid. Kinda like her.

But what about a cure? Well, so far, Chloe hadn't thought that far. She was resigned that this was, like, a part of her that might not heal. She thought she'd just have to deal with her FD forever. Maybe her FD was, like, DNA? But if the FD was genetic there hadn't been any indication she shared symptoms with any other Wong or Leiberman.

Plus, to look at her FD as something that needed to be cured only made it all seem worse—as if by acknowledging any intrinsic pathology to this desire-to-style-strangers-then-comment-on-their-wardrobe-aloud-thing implied she had something totally unfixable, damaged, alien, irreparable—that *she* herself was totally unfixable, damaged, alien, irreparable—a big ol' all-around DON'T. Ironically, however, Chloe was the first and only one to diagnose, and thus, pathologize, herself.

By this time, at the ripe old age of seventeen and a quarter and under increasing pressure to get a postgrad plan, all her fashion disorder symptoms were getting worse. Her FD was something that, like, not only had become a fixed part of her quirky mind but also was growing into something she could no longer keep to herself.

"You'll never quit so long as you stay with Dante. He's always been a terrible influence."

Spring enjoyed stating the obvious.

Chloe would've tried to defend Dante but she was distracted by Spring's new Eden Prep dolphin shorts—worn during another grueling three-hour crew practice.

Spring sure was a glutton for punishment. Crew, soccer, lacrosse, you name it she played it, and well, whether she wanted to or not and usually because her parents told her she had to or else.

"Did you really sew this pillow?" Spring cooed. "The sequins are amazing!"

"They're paillettes but whatever. Thanks."

"But you made it, like, in a day?" Spring pressed.

"Yeah, but pillowcases are the easiest thing to make, Spring. It's not, like, *couture.*"

"But I can't even sew a button!" Spring exclaimed.

"And," she continued, "I never would've figured out how to cut up my old Eden Prep T without wrecking it. It's totally fitted and cute now because of you!"

Was the token flattery just to get their friendship back on track? Or did Spring mean it? It was hard to tell lately since Chloe and Spring *were* drifting apart.

Mitchell incest aside, Spring was always glued to the pre-SC-Kappa Kappa Kappa crew (hi, gross) and all those Eden Prepsters, like, shared the same brain and boyfriend. And even if Spring wasn't exactly like those girls she sure spent plenty of QT with them instead of Chloe—prepping for nationals or some meet or Las Madrinas deb function.

For real, Spring would never stray from the designer staples of Wells Park to scour racks at the Swap Meet with Chlo anyhow. This was a sad but true realization especially when Chloe considered all the important history she and Spring shared up and down Avocado Lane. Just thinking about it made Chloe feel all sentimental and bummed out.

"I'll customize for you anytime, Spring Bean."

Spring smiled, relieved. "Spring Bean" or plain "Bean" had been Chlo's nickname for her ever since she suddenly shot up like a sunflower second semester of sixth grade. Practically overnight the girl grew, like, six inches, towering over Chlo like a willowy bean that could be snapped in two.

Spring's wide and pleasant face always looked

happy (even if she wasn't), and her swanlike neck was topped with a crown of flaxen, effervescent locks. Since she usually donned an apple green Lacoste sweater set (a style, mind you, practically identical to Eden Prep uniform), she really did look like a sunflower: yellow on top and green on the bottom, real agile and perky.

"So you're not mad about the Mitchell thing?" Spring hid her face in a deconstructed catalog Chloe had apparently cut up. She liked to draw over the models with what she would have preferred them to wear.

"Spring, I'm much more concerned with how embroidery and sewing will never be assets on a UC app. And even if they were, it's too late to dress my way into *any* college now."

"What are you talking about?"

Chloe was about to confess when she heard the sudden sound of distinct, choppy footsteps slapping the steps. Smoke still floating between them, she and Spring exchanged mutual "oh shit" looks.

"Pau-Pau!" Chloe cried, mouth exploding with smoke. She stubbed the flickering butt hard, and then, a thundering knock.

"Chloee-girl! Chlooe-girl, you inside?"

Pau-Pau's signature blue house slippers could be seen underneath the door, the only footwear she'd ever seemed to don since moving in. Not bad for a diabetic grandma who just had her esophagus removed and stood all of four feet five, hair included.

"Just a minute, Pau-Pau. I'm . . . I'm changing again."

Frantic, Spring scrambled to grab a can of raspberry mist. She began to spray in staccato bursts, then practically dumped the whole bottle onto the floor. The girls began to wheeze as an overwhelming berry vapor polluted the room.

"Why you need change five times, Chlooe-girl? You only Chinese girl change more times than whole Canton village!

"Pau-Pau smells smoke. Are yoou smoking, Chloe-girl?" She might have been seventy-three but she could smell a covered-up cigarette a mile away.

Chloe fanned the air with a giant throw pillow.

"No way, Pau," Chloe lied. "It's just a chem experiment that exploded, uh, with smoke. It's nada."

Please don't bust me. . . .

"Well, your ma want you right now," Pau muttered.

"Something about her lo-fan cooking. Pau-Pau refuse to help cook lo-fan food for Chinese holiday." She spat this in singsong Cantonese, high-pitched and squeaky.

"OK, I'll be downstairs in five minutes." Chloe popped a handful of Altoids in her mouth.

The knocking stopped. Apparently Pau-Pau was over it, already shuffling back down the steps while her signature backless slippers, her tat-tat-high (remember—check the glossary!), echoed loudly throughout the hall.

The girls exhaled in mutual relief and Chloe went to shut the windows. Below her, a long shadow loomed across the lawn. Lucinda was spying. Again. And teetering so far over the garden hedge she looked ready to fall over flat in her, yep, little peach Chanel flats. Binoculars clandestinely tucked into her matching wicker gardening basket, she was honing in on her newest target: the buxom neighbor who'd just moved in across the street. As in, the real-live-*Countess* neighbor with the thirteen hottie mover minions who, apparently, was hosting *her own* welcome party to coincide with the Chinese New Year!

"And to think, Lupe, she's not even Chinese. What business does she have throwing a Chinese New Year soiree?"

Lupe opted not to respond and silently clipped roses from a bush.

"Just keep pruning! This way I won't look bad."

Didn't her mom have better things to do than spy on the new neighbor? Like cook? And poor old Lupe. Sometimes Chloe thought it would be better if immigration did come and take her away.

And then Chloe witnessed a sight she would never forget. This Countess-person herself emerged, almost, like, poured out, from two enormous sliding glass doors, little decked-out attendant in tow. Chloe could have sworn a plume of yellow smoke floated in her wake as she strutted down a set of white marble stairs, a chapel-length silk-satin train sailing behind her and held up, yes, by a real, live somebody! A real, live somebody was holding her chapel-length silk-satin train as she prepared to cross Avocado Lane!

Chloe was intrigued. If only she had a closer view. She'd like to chat it up with a real, live Countess and ask how many wardrobe changes she required each day.

"Mrs. Leiberman!" the Countess called. "Ooh, a sack dress a la Balenciaga! How refreshing. What one sacrifices in shape one gets in space . . . space to breathe, no?"

Lucinda froze like a deer. The Countess was all red lips to here and buxom ta-tas to *there* and her hair was like Medusa's with a distinct gray tendril bouncing amid the velvety black curls.

"Well, good afternoon, dahling. I know it is last-minute but I wanted to invite you and Stanford to my little shindig up at the casita. 'Tis the Year of the Tiger so of course I just had to throw a party. I look very good in tiger, you know."

The mute attendee, a butler of sorts, gently set down her chapel-length silk-satin train and unscrolled an exquisite silk-screened fan, literally printed onto a fine leaf of silk. It was even trimmed in yellow crepe de chine braids and tied together with ivory fan sticks.

The center of the fan depicted the Countess, in repose, awash in a design of dragonflies and water lilies. Three sheets of vanilla-scented vellum were tucked into the folds, Chinese characters hand calligraphied on each. The center piece was in tiny, curly script and looked just like this:

> *La Contessa Coco l'Orange*
> *would just love you to attend the first of*
> *many events of the season to welcome both*
> *her glorious arrival to Wells Park and*
> *the Chinese New Year. This year we*
> *welcome back the magnificent Tiger.*
>
> *Dress Code: White Tie Animal, but of course.*

White tie animal? But there was no such thing! And no one in Wells Park celebrated the Chinese New Year except for the Wong-Leibermans! Simply vexed, Lucinda politely excused herself and marched away.

It was definitely time for a change, I mean, for Chloe to change outfits. But first, she'd have to take another Polaroid. A longstanding symptom, Chloe Polaroided her clothes at least once a day. She just had to. It was like, Polaroiditis.

Plus, Chloe hated to look at her entire reflection in one piece so she just photographed her clothes, and in parts. No matter how hard she tried Chloe felt like she would never go together for real. She thought she'd always look scrappy and strange. Oh, and definitely unhot.

Which brings us back to Dante. Until Chloe met Dante on the eve of her fifteenth birthday she never felt like anyone noticed her at all, let alone heard anyone tell her she was hot. (An overrated compliment for sure but at the time it did wonders for her imagined bad complexion.) Rumor had it people told Chloe she was cute, or at least said she had cute clothes plenty— but, like, something got lost in translation. Not until the words "Chloe, you're so fucking hot" came dripping from Dante's seemingly-all-too-sincere lips, soft and full and so easy to kiss, did she ever, ever consider herself appealing to look at, let alone h-o-t.

At present, Chloe Leiberman looked like this:

Her hair definitely looked Chinese, shiny and raven, but the texture was coarse, like her dad's borderline Jewish-fro. Her eyes were light brown like her dad's but they were almond shaped like her mom's. She was short like both parents but not really thick like him or thin like her. Basically, she was split down the middle, or rather, in thirds. She likened herself to a three-part picture puzzle she assembled and took apart constantly, rearranging the disparate pieces trying to make them feel whole. She never quite did feel like a whole person until she got dressed.

Chloe had decided to go with a military slash athletic theme, kinda Asian style. At first she thought wearing something old was anti the spirit of the Chinese New Year, a holiday where traditionally you're supposed to wear something new. But, like, her tried-and-true camouflage pants were silk, which is very Chinese, and the look would be new since she had never worn these pieces in this particular way. She figured it was an acceptable compromise.

Chloe slung the floods low around her narrow hips and secured them with a wide strip of hot-pink canvas. It was a makeshift belt with a giant gold buckle she'd bought on a sixth-grade discovery trip to Sacramento. (A class excursion where she *did* discover the joy of chunky quartz and hammered gold.)

She had cataloged sixty-three buckles next to her seventy-six pairs of shoes, all with mini pics stickered to their original boxes for easy reference. This buckle had an engraved dragon breathing fire—in keeping with her Asian theme.

To try to keep the peace with Lucinda, Chloe added her favorite shrunken warm-up jacket, well worn and frayed, over her "un-fancy" paint-splattered "Go Lakers!" T. You know, the one that really read "Ole!" since most of the letters were faded—something she and her other best friend, Sue Arriza, thought was rad. Chloe zipped it right below the ta-tas, as Sue's mom liked to call them, although Chloe preferred to call them denadas, since, for real, that was what they were.

Chloe switched the leather cuff for some black and white plastic bangles, added a charm bracelet with a peace symbol, and refastened a pearl choker around her neck since her mom just loved pearls. Slipping into four-inch satin peeptoes, new ones (but that she and Spring had sprayed metallic gold), Chloe snapped a picture, omitting her face from the frame, naturally, and felt complete.

"What's tonight's theme?" Spring asked, looking up from her magazine.

Chloe lit up. She loved to discuss themes.

"A tribute to the Chinese New Year! A holiday about letting go of the old so you can, like, let in the new but still mix up both. That's why I'm doing a vintage-inspired thing but in a new way."

Spring looked totally perplexed. "But how do the Lakers fit in?"

"It's my Ode to Team Sports but Not," Chloe explained.

"But you don't like sports, Chlo."

"It's supposed to be, like, ironic, Spring."

"Ohhhh . . ." Spring nodded, not exactly getting the point.

"Bean," Chloe ventured, "of course I don't *do* team sports for real. Or . . . football players who could practically be my younger brother."

"Jeez, Chloe, we're not doing anything! And what was that about sewing and embroidery not being assets on an app? They certainly are assets on a design school app—especially for Central Saint Martins. Right?"

Sure . . . If Chloe were to apply *for real* which she wasn't about to do.

"Spring Bean, you know fashion school's NOT on the Wong-Leiberman list even if it was the *only* school on mine. So . . . I decided not to apply anywhere."

Spring's jaw fell, To. The. Floor.

"But it's January, Chloe! Did you honestly not mail in *any* college apps? And, like, when were you planning on sharing this vital info with me?"

Chloe felt so guilty she just wanted to crawl back into her closet and dieee. Actually, she felt strangely compelled to go shopping for vintage thermals online. No doubt, breaking the latest to her family would be much more difficult than breaking it to Bean. It was a good thing Chloe opted for camo tonight cuz this was certainly gonna be war.

La Bomba

DO: Drop bombs in camouflage

DON'T: Think camouflage will let you hide a thing

The sprawling oak table was set for a king and his court—or, at least, like, the UN. A violated duck held center stage, fanned out on a silver tray, stuffed with tiny berries and leaves. Stacks of dumplings, latkes, cheese rolls, brisket, white rice, and bok choy exploded from fanciful dishes still gleaming with polish. Pale blue and white china perched atop giant gilded chargers. Monogrammed napkins, starched and militant, lined up next to the plates—blanched so white you wouldn't dare use one to actually wipe your mouth. Chloe was sandwiched between Zeyde and Pau, Stan and Lucinda sat at opposing heads of the table, and Mitchell sprawled out solo, for some reason meriting an entire side to himself.

Crystal goblets overflowed with apple cider (the Wong-Leibermans' was strictly a nonalcoholic home), and Mitchell raised a glass for a toast. He puffed out his chest, pectoral muscles well defined under an emerald green cashmere vest, various patches for team sports and clubs and accolades adorning the sides. Less the double-breasted blazer (tan for spring, navy for fall) Mitchell was still wearing his school uniform. His vest was layered over a baby pink oxford, sleeves rolled up twice on each side to display his tanned forearms, manicured nails, and prized Cartier tank watch. The special holiday merited a special bow tie of course, and his khakis (double reverse pleat, ew!) were of course in top form, immaculate and wrinkle free. His brown woven belt matched his brown Top-Siders, which he wore sans socks. Sans socks! What was up with this Euro-metrosexual detail? Chloe wouldn't be surprised if her brother slept like this—just in case the proverbial camera still rolled.

"First and foremost," Mitchell began, "I'd like to thank our present administration for rescuing the American economy from the former spendthrift liberal regime."

"Oy, jesus, here we go."

Tiny beads of sweat began to run down Zeyde's cheeks. Zeyde featured quite the bold fashion statement tonight: tan nylon track pants paired with an "It's Sergio" track jacket, label in bold energetic stripes, definitely circa 1993 and not quite old enough to be cool. Not to be underdressed, he topped the look off with a well-worn corduroy blazer, almond colored and frayed at the seams.

"This great administration," Mitchell continued, "has ensured that the good life in Wells Park will not only be possible, but will continue to flourish."

Zeyde furiously patted himself dry with a well-loved and -used hankie, pulled from the aforementioned corduroy blazer pocket.

"Chloe doll," he lamented, "my heart really could just plotz at such, forgive me for swearing, such chozzerai."

Chloe nodded amicably even though she knew *that* was total chozzerai. If anyone's heart was weak for real, it was Pau's—not Zeyde's. But more importantly, should she wear silver bangles tomorrow or gold?

"A toast to the elders! To Zeyde, he who hath set forth the illustrious tone for the entire Leiberman family to aspire toward and beyond! And to Pau, an exemplary model of courage and strength. We give thanks to Lord Buddha for her quick and smooth recovery. Welcome to our home."

Buddha? Since when had the young Republican started invoking Buddha? And if he paid any attention to anyone other than himself he would know that Pau was in remission—which, hello, is not the same thing as being recovered!

"A toast to my father! Not just my father, but my mentor too. I thank you from the bottom of my heart for teaching me not only how to meet but also how to exceed that bottom line. To our growing portfolios!"

"L'chayim!" Stan cried, raising a frosted glass high.

"And, lastly, to my radiant mother." Mitchell mused. "Oh where shall I begin? Thank you for this festive meal—yet another culinary achievement to add to the ever-growing list."

Lucinda blushed. "This? This was nothing," she pooh-poohed. Lucinda didn't do compliments well. They made her very uncomfortable.

"Eh-em," Mitchell coughed. "I suppose I should offer a toast to my sister. . . ."

Not one to ever lack for words, Mitchell suddenly appeared confused. Chloe made up her mind. Tomorrow, it would be all about gold. Aztec, drapey, beaded gold.

"Mitchelllaah, fi-di-la!" Pau-Pau cried, tapping a glass impatiently.

"Yesss. Let's see. I suppose I can thank you, Chloe, for keeping the gossip lively at Eden Prep and the house, well, well entertained. Oh, and for having hot friends like Spring."

So it was true! They really did go public! She debated whether to toss the cider in his face now or later and chalk it to the evening's "entertainment," but Stan interrupted her thoughts.

"Well then, before we dig in, why don't you add something to Mitch's toast, Chloe—which by the way, son, was quite impressive."

Chloe gulped. She suddenly forgot how to speak English altogether. Five pairs of eyes switched to her and her heart began to pound. All she could do was stare vacantly into her bowl, twirling and twirling her silver spoon, until the only thing she saw inside her tureen was a tiny version of herself, drowning in the low-carb, wheat-free matzoh ball soup. She saw herself dressed in ancient prison black and whites, tiny skull-cap pulled over her small ears, clutching a tin bowl in a cold cell while dark iron bars clamped down, all around, all around. *Wait a sec,* she thought, this skull-cap could be kinda cute if it was paired with a billowy peasant skirt, a red one, hand embroidered, say, with cockatoos and—

"Lots of slashed ruffles. Definitely gold."

Mitchell snickered. Lucinda cringed. Stan looked totally concerned.

"With my trusty white Cons," she whispered, staring far, far away.

"What a luftmensh, this one," Zeyde declared. "Head always up in the clouds."

Chloe would wear this new look Monday! As a tattered yet triumphant Ode to Having Survived the Holiday Meal!

"Chloe-girl, hi-yaaa!" Pau-Pau cried. "Pau-Pau don't have nine live."

"Sorry, Pau." Chloe shifted uncomfortably in her

seat, like she had an irritating loose thread that needed to be cut off. Actually, *she* felt like an irritating loose thread that had been, like, unraveling for seventeen and a quarter years and just had to be cut-the-fuck-off-now. . . .

"Well, Chloe Wong," Lucinda spat, "answer your father, for heaven's sake!"

Chloe inhaled deep. "All right then. But I should preface what I'm about to say by thanking everyone in the family first, especially Mitch."

Mitchell appeared confused. Chloe almost felt, like, sorry for the burden he carried in his perfect khaki pockets.

"Thanks, Mitch," Chloe began, "for always being such a model Eden Prepster and Wong-Leiberman. At least one of us will be going to college and you can all guess who that one is because Ididn'tmailinany-applicationsandIforgottotaketheSATstoo. Like, Amen, or rather, Gung Hay Fat Choy."

Chloe wasn't sure who reacted first. It was all one giant, multilingual gasp. Cider spilled, bok choy flew, and a lambasting cry all merged as one. Even Wally stopped eating and poked a curious head up from his "fancy" bowl—you know, one of those elevated feeders so he didn't have to, like, exert his neck or anything.

"That's real funny, Chlo," Mitch braved. "Like I said, prime-time reality entertainment."

"Bu—but I distinctly recall you took the SATs three times with Spring," Lucinda stammered.

. . . Not reaally. Attempt #1: She had been out uber-late with Dante. Attempt #2: She was bidding all night on vintage online. Attempt #3: She was just kinda over attempting it.

"But you promised us you mailed and certified all your applications back in November! Surely you mailed at least one application . . . a state, safety school even?"

What was so safe about college anyhow?

"Well, that's just great!" Zeyde wailed. "To be a luftmensh is one thing, but to be a schlemiel who thinks she doesn't need college, absolute meshugge!"

"For once, Zeyde, I actually agree." Lucinda clutched the sides of the table tight and restrained herself from hurling her plate of leafy bok choy and parboiled duck straight at Chlo. But then, Stan totally freaked.

Stanley slammed the table so hard even the chandelier shook and swayed, threatening to, like, decapitate any unlucky victim of his sudden wrath!

"I do NOT bill four hundred dollars an hour so my daughter can wind up a bum on the street!" he roared. "And the street is exactly where'll you'll be, missy, once I'm through with you!"

Chloe swallowed hard. Couldn't they, like, discuss this situation? Other options—B-list schools—C-list even! On the streets? That was harsh. Her dad, like, never took it there.

"I'm sorry, Daddy," Chlo mumbled.

"Sorry? Sorry just isn't good enough!"

Stan's entire face swelled up and turned to a shade of red Chloe had never seen erupt on human flesh.

"You, Chloe Wong, are a liar!"

Liar? More like a good editor . . .

"We paid good money for you to take that Princeton Review, two times I believe, and you don't even take the exam?!"

"But I knew I'd do badly. I don't test well so I forgot, honest."

Well, that part was true—the part about not testing well.

"So you just thought the solution was not to take the SATs at all—thereby wasting my money and mocking me in the process?!"

Jeez. Why was this about him? He already went to college, a really good and hard one at that!

"We have let you get away with murder, absolute MURDER. First, we say nothing when you 'transfer out' of Eden Prep, an unthinkable travesty. Then we say nothing when you take up with that, that—pervert of a boyfriend who's hopped up on god-only-knows what kind of drugs—"

"You mean the schvartz?" Zeyde hollered, "There are drugs too!"

Chloe shook her head, totally mortified. How could Zeyde bust out with the word "schvartz" and think it was kosher!

"Well about this 'urban' preying-mantis-pedophile we say nothing, we just let you 'hang out.' *And* we say nothing even now while you carouse about town with that Mexican girl—"

"Colombian," Chloe corrected.

"What difference does it make? She whores through

the neighborhood in clothes that would make my poor mother roll in her grave and you have some chutzpa to correct me in the middle of a lecture!"

"But Mexico is a totally different country than Colombia and Sue's part Italian."

Stan slammed his fists down again.

"You don't know when to quit! Or actually, I stand corrected. You quit everything that you should not!"

This was valid. Chloe Wong-Leiberman *was* an avid quitter. Viola, dance, track . . . and field. A borderline C student when she could've got A's, she was a quasi-underachiever fully comfortable with being average. Neither a leader nor a follower, she never quite lived up to her much-touted "potential." She had always been smart according to teachers but never "applied herself" seriously. And no matter what her friends said to make her feel better about her FD she just couldn't justify that thinking about clothing, even if it was in an obsessive way, really qualified in the applying-herself category.

"And now, Ms. Wong-Leiberman, on the Chinese New Year, no less, a day for our family to come together and celebrate our rich heritage, you decide to ruin it by casually mentioning that you 'forgot' to take the SATs and didn't apply to a single goddamn college! A decision which means you will live out the rest of your days like some bum hawking shmatte with the Gypsies downtown! You, Chloe Wong-Leiberman, have disgraced this family. And you have broken my heart."

Stanley looked about ready to die of some spontaneous epileptic babbling seizure right there, foaming at the mouth all over his prized Hawaiian shirt! (which wouldn't have been so bad). He was shvitzing and shaking all over like the San Andreas itself.

Mitchell's jaw could've snapped off his body at any sec, a la Spring. Zeyde's face was buried deep in his hands. And Lucinda sat frozen as carbo-lite.

But Pau-Pau hopped up, chopstick pointed like a sword.

"Enough, fai-ji!" she spat.

"Good GAWD, Moth-er!" Lucinda cringed. "Pleeeeze sit down!"

"Mo lay yel, Lucindaaa. Cra-zy bok-gui. Enough!"

"Um, like, may I please be excused?" Chloe whispered to no one in particular.

Her arms and legs shook and swayed like the San Andreas too. She had done it. For real.

Chloe had dropped the bomb and killed her family.

part two

Indicate a person who has had a significant influence on you, and describe that influence

[Didn't Chloe just do that? *Oh,* you mean in a good way.]

Pre-Party Palazzo Pjs

[Person number one:
La Contessa Coco l'Orange]

DO: Wear four-inch heels for special occasions

DON'T: Wear four-inch heels if you, like, have to walk

Sure she was trespassing but Chloe just couldn't help herself. She loved the thrill of illegal entry. It was as if she was literally being pulled across the street by some invisible yet inevitable magnet.

She had to get in.

Into the Villa, that is. The Villa de la Contessa. You know, the not-so-humble abode of the mysterious buxom lady who was hosting that not-so-humble

Chinese New Year soiree. Talk about a scandal. The entire neighborhood couldn't stop blabbing about what this *supposed* Countess supposedly did to supposedly come into her supposed wealth.

The rumors were wild. She was from Beirut. She was a frequent divorcée. She was a kept woman. She was a Countess through marriage, but after that divorce she got to keep the title and three homes—including the home across the street, making her the first outsider to arrive on the Wells Park scene in well over a decade. Her name in full was the Countess Coco l'Orange. La Contessa, for short.

It was about time Chloe checked out the real deal for herself.

Chloe assessed the entrance situation. It was all high security in front, in back, and along the sides, prepping for red-carpet arrivals. Then there was all that topiary—topiary this and that for days. Hmmm. How to secure entry without snagging her silk or wrecking her heels and, for that matter, SANS invite? She could take her pants off for a small sec (she was wearing cute boy shorts), but with her luck Peter Windemere would jump out from behind a bush and snap a photo. He was, like, her stalker.

Removing her shoes would do for now as she prepared (a) to hop a fence, or (b) to squeeze on past a topiary swan. She opted for b—sliding right between the swan and what looked like some massive topiary David. She almost snagged a silk pocket in the process, but thank GAWD, emerged unscathed.

She was in.

Chloe's jaw dropped to the floor, or rather, the marble. Before her, the grounds swept back and forth in every direction. So it really was some re-created Greco-Roman-revival temple thing happening out here! White on white—like the steps leading to Caesar's itself. (This just vexed Lucinda to no end. After all, Greek revival didn't GO with Avocado Lane! Avocado Lane was strictly an American colonial kind of street.)

Adding to an already obscene list of DON'Ts was the rotunda situation. The woman *had the gall* to paint her enormous open-aired rotunda flanked by hundred-foot-high Corinthian columns cherry *red!* AND this cherry red rotunda positioned itself smack dab in front of and above the Beckett home not only making it the "gauchiest" property on the block but also making it the most elevated, overtaking at least three Well Parkers' entire ocean views.

And then, Chloe was struck—blinded by the light! Or, like, by a statuesque figure glittering up ahead. With languid arms stretched out in the enormous open-aired cherry red rotunda also perfectly framed by gigantic twin palms, La Contessa, the Countess Coco l'Orange, emerged as if from a dream. She was standing alone like the queen of the world, basking in the 360-degree glow of the tranquil Pacific decked out in full-on pre-party palazzo pjs! Waving a long, golden cylinder that she alternately raised to her parted lips, then, in one single exasperated motion, dropped to her side, the Countess appeared to be smoking a fake cigarette. She slouched against a hundred-foot-high Corinthian column, all nonchalant, with a floor-length coat of some endangered species casually tossed across a shoulder. Chloe just couldn't contain herself.

"Is that coat, like, for real?" she blurted.

"Of course it's real," the Countess snapped, more offended by the question than the crasher. "I don't do fakes."

Fur, not faux? It was, like, seventy-five degrees. Chloe respected her already—the type of woman who suffered for the cause.

She descended from the rotunda while un-smoking her fake cigarette, palazzo pjs blowing in the breeze. They were yellow silk, a sumptuous one-piece confection, and they billowed wide through the legs over four-inch gold braided mules. Chloe just had to gawk. She had never seen a woman in so much fur and fringe and rocks—previewed in such a dazzling array of colors and sets and styles! Even the Countess's fingernails had rocks. They were like ruby red talons, the tips of each studded with a different stone.

Chloe slipped her peeptoes back on, feeling terribly underdressed and quite apologetic. I mean, she was standing face to face with the real, live, breathing Countess herself! As in the Countess whose image had preceded the real thing in a totally epic way! Had she known they would meet wardrobe to wardrobe she would've changed to mark the occasion.

"I see we're sneaking out for a cig, young thing," the Countess purred.

Chloe took offense. She hadn't even left with her "cigs," thank you very much.

"Actually I was just—"

"Breaking and entering!" the Countess cried, inching close. She smelled like jasmine and cherries—an intoxicating scent.

"Was not! Like, I got kicked out of my house, so I was going for a walk, which I quite honestly hate to do but, like, had no choice since my car was taken away. And I don't smoke unless I'm wearing my smoking sweatshirt which clearly I'm not."

"Come here, young thing." The Countess beckoned. "Let me take a lookie-loo at your shooooz."

She raised a jade-framed monocle up to what seemed to be yellow eyes—just like a LYNX—as in the supple, creamy, REAL LYNX coat she had wrapped around her.

"They remind me of a pair Roger made my mother years ago—" she mused. "Shoes like sculpture, that Monsieur Vivier, reaaally. Tell me, are they old or new?"

"Um, they're kinda new but not. I bought them at a store but they weren't right so I hand-painted them gold."

"Hmmm. So you're an artist then?" The Countess examined Chlo's shoes close, strands of pearls glittering amid gemstones in an ample décolletage.

Chloe blushed. "Oh god no. I'm just a senior, at Roosevelt. This really easy lame school. And no, like, I don't have any postgrad plans so please don't ask about them."

"Planzzz are terribly overrated," the Countess cooed. "I try never to plan anything at all! Except for my little Chinese New Year shindig I'm hosting later tonight, that is. Perhaps you and . . . your *father* would like to attend?"

Stanley? Was the Countess, like, jocking her dad?

Ew.

"Thanks so much for the invite but I'll definitely be under house arrest on account of me not having a plan—like to go to college—something I broke to the fam tonight. I was actually kinda kicked out. For real. I might be homeless. And even if I were to sneak out which I'll probably end up doing anyhow cuz I'm always grounded I don't have anything appropriate to wear."

Chloe suddenly felt exposed and wanted to go home and change. And then, her phone rang. Pau-Pau?

"Oh, hey, Pau. What's up?"

"Chlooe-guurl. Your chi-sen-pau need you buy Tiger Balm, tit da jow, Seven-Eleven."

Tiger Balm?

"Gao-chaw, Pau? Like, I was kicked out, remember?"

"Hui! Pau need you drive. Your bok-gui father left."

"But what about Mitch?"

"Mitchella, mo-yung!"

For real. But, like, she didn't really want to have to drive her grandmother to 7-Eleven to buy "ointment" for god knows what orifice. Plus what if this was a trap?

"I'm not so sure I can, Pau."

"Chlooe-guurl, Pau-Pau say time come home!" she clucked. "Go for ride. Then Pau show you how sew welt pocket—hui, five-pocket jean."

Click.

Pau hung up.

Well, all right. Chloe did need help with welt pockets. But traditionally they didn't even go on five-pocket jeans? What was Pau talking about? Chloe flipped her phone shut.

"Sorry, but I've got to go buy Tiger Balm for my grandma—she just got out of the hospital but she's all right."

The Countess continued to study Chloe with her yellow cat eyes, quite amused.

"Tiger Balm?" she inquired.

"Yeah, Tiger Balm. It's, like, this weird cure-all Chinese ointment. I know it's random but she doesn't drive or wear anything you can, like, actually feature in public. Well—at least ever since she moved in."

And got cancer . . . Chloe started to shvitz nervously. This Countess lady sure was coming close, still puff-puffing away on her fake cigarette.

"Um, well, it's been lovely meeting you, Ms. . . ."

"Just call me La Contessa!" she exclaimed. "I think I'll have Julius send for you after school sometime. He's my number one schmo."

And away she went—swiveling past the open-air

cherry red rotunda, billowing satin palazzo pjs swishing and swaying across the sweeping marble steps.

Hmm. Maybe dropping bombs worked in Wells Park after all. (And also, why did every Chinese pau under the sun swear by Tiger Balm? What exactly was Tiger Balm anyhow?)

Every Day Is Like Sunday

[Person Number Two (and Three!):
Sue and Rosy A.]

DO: Aspire to look like you feel

DON'T: Be so obvious you, like, have to talk about how you feel

Technically, Chloe was grounded until much, much further notice. Quelle surprise. But today she had a three-hour get-out-of-450-Avocado-Lane pass under the sole condition she would be studying with Spring, but I mean, didn't her mom know by now? Chloe never told her the truth. She was going to Sue's.

Sue Arriza had been Chloe's *other* best friend since her first day at Roosevelt High, the very first time

Chloe Wong-Leiberman ever stepped foot on public school soil.

It was like this.

Chloe was wearing a black fedora, a white tank top, and a pair of green Dickies over white shell-toe Adidas. A group of cholas got in her face walking to fifth period. They cornered her and asked the question she had been asked, like, too many times to count. "Where you from, girl?" their ringleader demanded. Chloe couldn't tell you her name but she could tell you her breath smelled like cherries and she wore these fantastic twizzly earrings that grazed her broad shoulders. Chloe complimented them even, but suggested she wear them with a different neckline.

Aloud.

Right then and there tiny Sue Arriza jumped in to defend. Chloe had rescued Sue's beloved hoodie earlier that morning after the zipper totally busted. She had pinned it back together into this rad capelet instead, a crafty save that Sue would never forget in light of the total emergency. Plus, she liked Chloe's style and wanted to check the new prep-school ex-pat out.

The cholas stepped back and have respected Chloe ever since. Chlo didn't know it at the time but tenth-grader Sue Arriza carried lots of clout thanks to her mom, Rosy, the most respected Santera in the hood. Ever since bonding over buying wife beaters at Wal-Mart two years ago, they've been inseparable.

Today, Chloe was feeling nostalgic and all alone

and kinda sorry for herself which is why she opted for a blouson tube dress in lemon jersey, something breezy and oversized: An Ode to Easier, Softer Times. With rainbow-laced espadrilles, gigantic Jackie Os to shield herself from the sun, and an elbow-length stack of chunky bangles to hear and feel clanking about, Chloe was practically swimming in the dress and the bracelets and shades but she, like, needed the space.

Chloe felt sick to her core. She didn't exactly enjoy lying to her parents but they really gave her no other choice! They didn't even try to understand who she was so why should she bother telling them the truth? Plus, it was all too apparent she was a *part* of a family she'd never feel a *part* of at all. Like, Chloe was convinced she was more space alien than Wong-Leiberman.

Sorry, folks, we DON'T do returns or exchanges.

Not store policy.

Ever since that ill-fated Chinese New Year night Chloe's mom had totally ignored her and Stan had been MIA. Mitchell was gloating in all the Chloe-sucks glory and Zeyde clucked his teeth for shame every time they crossed paths in the kitchen. This meant Chloe communicated with the Wong-Leibermans through Pau, a bit of a challenge but at least it gave them QT alone to sew.

They sewed upstairs in Pau's attic apartment, a nice place to hide and practice her pretend portfolio, a collection Chloe was working on even if at that time she thought she'd never get to apply to Saint Martins for real.

But back to Rosy and Sue. They lived in El Conejo, what Wells Parkers called the ghetto. But Chloe felt safer in the Arriza casita than in any patrolled estate in Wells Park. For real. The cozy cottage always smelled like fried chicken and baby powder and honeysuckle and something sweet like tobacco mixed with caramel. Toddlers always waddled around the meandering yard since in addition to being a rad Santera, Rosy ran a little day-care center from the house. She was, like, the Queen of Multitasking.

The winter day was unusually warm, even for El Conejo. The sweeping valley was always a good ten degrees warmer than Wells Park—sort of like a spiraling, sprawling pit that the sun relentlessly poured into and beat down. Nevertheless, Rosy Arriza's garden always seemed to grow. Her small grove of avocado and lemon trees was always ripe with fruit, and all around tomato plants and herbs and white flowers, gardenias to be exact, burst out here and there from little fountains.

The familiar circle of grass, the tiny pebbles on the path, the antique wooden knocker—all these things made Chloe feel relieved and reassured—like everything would somehow be OK. She imagined this was how it must feel to come home if you actually wanted to go there. Then she felt guilty and weird and nervously adjusted the elastic around her chest. Yep, her ta-tas as Rosy liked to call them were seriously de nadas, for real.

But before Chloe could even step inside the single-story Spanish, Sue rushed out. She was proudly featuring a flirty red circle skirt, pink Chuck Ts, and a hand-dyed signature wife beater, this one ruched at the sides with contrasting yellow ribbons. It was a detail Chloe had added and admired now. Sue could pull off everything from punk-rock chola to subversive and sweet because she, like, meant it.

"Finally. Let's go, space cadet!" Sue rolled her big green eyes—the one good thing her dad left her with since he took off when she was three and never came back. He was the Italian part—making Sue three parts Colombian and one part Italian. Sue was definitely a hottie who knew it but worked her hottie status not just to her advantage but yours too. (She really was a generous *and* resourceful girl.)

"Sorry, Sue-Lou. I was spacing and lost track of the time."

"It's healthy to daydream, hija." Mrs. A glid out of the house and planted a gigantic kiss on Chloe's cheek.

Chloe couldn't help but, like, kinda gawk. I mean, Rosy Arriza glowed just like the moon! She was a vision in silver and white, her beaded tunic paired over extralong white cotton batiste pants, with flat goddessy sandals featuring a dangling coral accent at the toe. Her hair bounced down the slope of her back in a single, perfect braid—swaying gently like a leaf. Why couldn't her mother's hair sway gently like a leaf?

"I'm sure you're the only adult who feels that way,

Mrs. A. Like, sometimes I think my kind of daydreaming might be hazardous to my health. It probably is a good thing my folks took my car away cuz I'm highly likely to cause a major accident—again. Are you coming shopping with us?"

"No, she's not," Sue said, hooking Chlo's arm. "She's working, big surprise. C'mon, Mama, keys please."

"Ai, hija. Calmate. First, I wanna hear what's going on with my other little star?"

Little star. Just hearing Rosy say that made Chloe wanna

curl

up

and

dieeee.

"Did you send in your application to fashion school yet? It's in London, right? How exciting! It's inspiring to wake up in the morning and see a different view."

"Ma-ma," Sue interjected. "Por favor. Like, will you leave her alone? Isn't it time for your next registro anyhow?"

Oh, so, registros were what Sue's mom was, like, famous for. In between running the day-care center she gave special readings called registros that were kinda like therapy but not and involved Santeria orishas, which are, like, gods of the Santeria faith. The orishas communicated through rad Santeras like Rosy—but that's a whole other story. Just know for now that it was a really big deal to get a registro from Rosa Maria Arriza.

"Mrs. A, my parents aren't too thrilled with that prospect, actually. Like, I'm not even allowed to apply."

"No te preoccupadas, little star. No worries. It'll all work out and you'll make the right choice. Your folks will see. No one can decide what's best for you—not even them. Ai, I should listen to my own words!"

She spun Sue round to hug her close, all zerberts and kisses.

Rosy always said or did things like that, sincere, but not, like, serious. That's probably why people came to her for advice since Rosy never seemed to worry or freak out. She usually let Sue do her own thing too—even if a choice might be a mistake—including Sue's recent decision slash "mistake" to wait to apply to college. Sue wanted to work on a vineyard in Naples and get back to her mystery dad's roots, punto. As in, Naples, *Italy*, not Naples, Florida. Waking up to a different view, for real. Sue was leaving on a jet plane right after graduation and no one was gonna stop her.

"Ma-ma, pleeeze!" Sue cried, buckled over at the waist while Rosy continued with the kissing flurry, something that was definitely more welcomed than dissed.

Chloe's mom never kissed her, like, ever. Chloe felt *just* a little jealous. Come to think of it, Lucinda never kissed anyone. *And if it was fine for Sue not to go to college yet then why was it so bad for Chloe not to go at all?*

"Ai, now I'm dizzy from all this kissing. OK, hijas, con cuidado por favor. Be careful on the 405. Oh, and it probably is better if Sue drives."

"Yeah, yeah. No worries, Mom. C'mon, Chlo. Let's go." Sue hurried Chloe down the path, pausing to pick up Chloe's discarded smoking sweatshirt. Chloe sometimes left it in the bushes when she was trying to quit.

"Since you won't be needing this anymore, Wong, can I borrow it?"

Sue tied the sweatshirt around her neck.

"I'll just make you one already!" Chloe exclaimed.

"Wong, if I had a dollar for every time you threatened to do that then I'd be rich like you!"

"I'm not rich, Sue, my dad is." She hated when Sue mentioned the difference in their "social" status even if there was *quite* a difference indeed. Like, Chloe felt ashamed for having money and guilty that Sue had none and uncomfortable and irritated that it was even an issue for her at all since it wasn't really an issue for Sue.

"You'd get rich too if you just sold your clothes, already. Prove to your parents there's a, whawould Mitch call it, a market."

"Sue-Lou, Stan and Lucinda still have yet to recover from the latest . . ."

"I think they'll get over it, Wong. Besides, today's the first day of the rest of your life! It's all good."

Sue smiled reassuringly, just like Rosy, whose gorgeous gauzy tunic was shining brightly in the sun. If only *Chloe* could wear life like one of Rosy's carefree cotton tunics—loose and embroidered by hand and flowing real easy when she walked, I mean when she "glid" (cuz she kinda glid more than walked).

Now that was something to aspire toward. For real.

Sacrifice

[Person Number Four: Pau]

DO: Sacrifice for the right cause

DON'T: Sacrifice just because

You could say things eventually got back to the yoosh at the Wong-Leiberman household.

Water polo and lacrosse were in full swing for Mr. All-Star Everything so Mitchell was always at some game or rally or party for the team. (Besides, free time was a Mitchell DON'T that might just give him too much time to think for himself.)

Currently, Stan and Zeyde were at war. Zeyde had shacked up with the infamous Christmas La Jolla "hunny," a plump little fan of control-top and hair-spray he met kibbitzing at one of his senior citizen pancake breakfasts. Stan was, to say the very least, perturbed by his dad's indiscretion.

The latest feud, however, couldn't have been all that tragic since Zeyde still made an every-so-often guest appearance. Chlo could hear him snoring—lying dead as a doorknob in his maroon poly blend "Pierre Cardin" or "It's Sergio" track suit, tiny patch of fur revealed above a woolen plaid or flesh-toned grandpa sock, like, gathered at a bony ankle—an orthopedic, gray sneaker—the "comfort" kind with soft, ventilated soles for "breathing," dangling at the foot of a four poster bed.

Ever since Chinese New Year, Lucinda hadn't said another word to Chloe about college, going to college, or anything else for that matter—electing to direct orders in monosyllabic sentences or notes through Lupe or Pau which was cool cuz Lupe never busted Chlo for smoking and Pau, well, she offered instructive, if unusual, company.

Every day way up in the attic Pau and Chloe would sit and sew something from Chloe's *pretend* Saint Martins portfolio, whose theme Chloe chose to entitle Five Cali Pieces. The app would have required her to submit, like, sketches only (she had them for months) but Pau insisted that Chloe make everything for real even if she wasn't applying to the school for real.

So while easy-listening favorites Linda Ronstadt or Kris Kristofferson played in the background, Pau nudged and prodded Chloe to hand-stitch hems (very therapeutic), perfect buttonholes (a bitch to do, for real), and finish seams (French ones, like, to prevent fraying).

All the Wongs and Leibermans, including Chloe, seemed to forget Pau was in remission from the C word. Even Pau forgot she had ever had the C word! Or, at least, she didn't act like a sick person with a C situation. They could, like, be in the middle of trimming threads when, all of a sudden, Chloe would turn and Pau would be gone—venturing the hood in her velour tat-tat-high, whistling loud to catch the bus. Either that or she'd be screaming "No whammies!" from the breakfast nook. She just loved the Game Show Network and, as bizarre as it might sound, telenovelas, which FYI are Latin soaps. Pau was doing all right adjusting to the Wong-Leiberman world thanks to Lupe and TiVo and maybe Chlo.

Chloe was working on An Ode to the Tiger. She draped some muslin over a dress form and thought about clashing patterns, hidden seams, stripes, and tangerines. She wasn't too sure if the Look would be a part of the original Five Cali Pieces or just a continuation of the theme but she felt inspired by the Chinese New Year and jeez, by Pau?

"Crap," she muttered, dropping another pin. The pin rolled along the creaky floorboard and came to a stop next to a bright lacquered dish. Peanut brittle and Andes mints were piled high atop slices of fresh ginger, twin satsumas, and a big stack of laysee, which,

FYI, means new money for a new year. The laysee was folded in bright red and gold envelopes stamped with the Chinese character double happiness, and you burned the envelopes to make offerings to ancestors and Buddha and stuff since they were supposed to bring you good luck. *Luck*. Something Chloe certainly lacked. She perched on her elbows staring at the New Year shrine, and, even though she felt kinda lame, made a wish.

"Chloee-girl! No time for fat-mung. Need one more look. Last look."

The Last Look. Something Chloe hadn't figured out quite yet.

She watched her grandmother's hands, plump and wrinkled and strong. Chloe pictured all the fabric that had passed through them—all the cheongsams Pau-Pau had pieced together—cut, trimmed, and sewed every day, maybe every night in that hidden sweat-shop (and it *was* a sweatshop) in Chinatown, many years before. A room she imagined, like, had no light, or had really bad fluorescent light. Not even a room but more like a hole—without a proper chair or anything—a hole where she probably made no more than a pinche buck an hour creating what was really couture while wearing some totally unflattering smock. No wonder her mom hated to sew. No wonder Lucinda hated Chloe to sew too. . . .

Huh. Something suddenly made sense.

"Hi-yaaa, luftming," Pau clucked.

Chloe giggled at her grandmother's latest uncon-ventional word choice. "You mean, luftmensh, Pau. No doubt I'm that. A luftmensh, or ming, or both." She planted a kiss on her grandmother's cheek and watched her hands maneuver and negotiate the folds with ease—the consistent hum of the machine zipping back and forth, back and forth, just like a lullaby.

"Chloe-girl, treat time for Pau-Pau. Sweet treat." She rubbed her belly and arched an eyebrow, all partner-in-crime like.

Chloe laughed and rolled her eyes.

"Hui, sur-jen! Only Oreo. Just five. Pau-Pau cut back."

Chloe looked at her little sewing machine and released the presser foot (you know, the part that latches onto the fabric). Then she went downstairs thinking about Pau-Pau's little altar and sacrifice and wished she could figure out a way to apply to Saint Martins for real.

part three

Extracurricular activities

[Do people and shopping count? How about shopping with people?]

El Conejo Swap Meet, the
Promenade, and Crystal Court

DO: Keep where you shop to yourself

DON'T: Keep to yourself while shopping

Chloe and Sue always went shopping on Sundays. It was like church. Or temple. Together they faithfully followed whatever flea market or swap meet was happening and this morning meant going to the El Conejo Swap Meet to process and review.

"Wong, you can't blame Spring for thinking Mitch is kinda hot—in a—Hey, what's that white guy's name? The one she likes to watch on TV with the bow tie?"

"Tucker Carlson and please don't encourage their twisted relationship."

Sue arched a lightly penciled brow in that you've-got-to-be-kidding-me-for-being-a-total-hypocrite kind of way.

"What?" Chloe asked, feigning ignorance, just like Spring. Sue arched her brow higher. "I know you were gonna call me a hypocrite but for real, Sue-Lou, I'm just, like, confused."

She hoped that shopping with Sue would help her get perspective. Shopping with Sue always helped Chloe get perspective. It was a goal-oriented, focused activity. Looking for that specific something she just *had* to find helped her feel together and in control. *Finding* that specific something made her feel accomplished and relieved. Chloe couldn't begin to make sense of her recent familial disgrace situation until she coordinated a new look. Then there was making sense of Dante, who hadn't called, texted, or e-mailed for four, make that five whole agonizing days! Now what was up with that?

"Yeah, Chlo. The public needs to know: Why do you *still* date that emo-punk-rock loser?" Sue tilted her head, Eden Prep style, clearly mimicking Spring. Chloe elbowed her to stop-it-already. Even though her two best friends came from completely different planets it really would help out if they could try to relate to each other. But after two trying years it was all too clear that neither Spring nor Sue was about to stray from comfort zones or home turf. Chloe, on the other hand, well, she never felt at home anyhow so it didn't really matter to her if she went back and forth. She was used to feeling in the middle, sometimes a part of one world, sometimes all alone in her own—kinda like a schizophrenic Ping-Pong ball never landing in one place. Or like a random-colored pair of shoes desperately seeking the right outfit to match, or rather unmatch, perfectly.

"How quickly you forget who introduced him to me," Chloe retorted. "And Dante's now a post-emo-punk-rock loser, remember?" They snickered at the distinction—something Dante was apt to point out lest he be lumped together with regular emo bands, a label he cringed at being labeled with.

Oh, the saga of Dante Spinoza: ongoing, tortured, no end in sight. Dante sure was dark and brooding, lead singer of the very dark and brooding emo-punk or rather the *post*-emo-punk band The Mourned.

Every time Dante smiled at her Chloe just melted and opened up completely. It was lame and embarrassing to admit, but for real. Like, Dante really saw who she was. He noticed what she wore and everything, commenting on key details like her new pink cocktail ring or a cool pair of mod tights, for example. And *he* told *her his feelings*—confessing his darkest and most tortured secrets which he then tried to write songs about. Dante even called Chloe his muse, which means she inspired his art thank you very much, and well, that just about *killed* Chloe with glee. Chloe never felt invisible or disposable or space alienish around Dante. Chloe felt seen and significant and, dare I say, special.

I mean, she was his *muse*?!

But, muse or not, Chloe and Dante were not a legal couple, which might be obvious given she was seventeen and he was twenty-six. Like, that's just not legal. Not like Chlo cared about what was legal or not but . . . she did care about all those red flags she was starting to see. It was a curious phenomenon, maybe part of her FD, and it had recently spread to him. Like, she was starting to see literal red flags pinned to his vintage Zeppelin Ts and French military caps, flapping about, from the Red Carpet, of course.

Red Flag #1: He's the lead singer in a band. Need I say more?

Red Flag #2: He smokes. Chloe's trying to quit. This means he's prone to other addictions too—a red flag times, at least, three!

Red Flag #3: He talks about himself or his car, this tricked-out '68 Charger (total agro-but-hot-dude car) for at least ten minutes before asking Chloe how she is. This means he is a self-obsessed NARCISSIST, which is definitely not a good thing even if Chloe can relate (to being self-obsessed, not to the Charger, she's more of an old Bronco kind of girl).

Red Flag #4: He never calls when he says he will. Flaky? Or is that just plain, old-fashioned LYING?

Red Flag #5: He's always late or doesn't show up at all and THEN acts like nothing out of the ordinary occurred—not exactly one to own up to things.

Red Flag #6: He sabotages everything good for him. For example, every time he's actually on the verge of getting signed after one of his trillion showcases he'll do something totally drastic like drive to Alabama or Kentucky and decide to raise chickens or something random like that . . . leaving the band, and Chlo, in his Charger dust.

Despite the obvious warning signs (I mean, literal red flags are pretty ob-vious), Chloe was in love. So she did what anyone else would do who's ever felt completely and totally and hopelessly in love; she ignored them all and hoped they'd eventually go away.

"I thought you guys broke up last week. *Again.*" Sue tried to say this all nonchalant. She realized she had a narrow window of opportunity here to contest Dante's latest bad boy behavior since she was the one, unfortunately, who hooked it all up. Who knew an intended one-time hookup with her cousin would turn into such the two-year saga? Dante and Chlo weren't actually supposed to, like, like each other and end up all tortured boyfriend slash girlfriend! And that was exactly-what-happened. She and Chloe had been discussing this complicated situation over a rack of shirred and fur-lined parkas, real Brooklyn ones Sue just adored.

"So I'm not too good with follow-through, Sue. Oh look, here's a good one." Chloe checked the lining of a puffy parka now. She would have to rip it out of course and sew in a new silk one in hot pink, Sue's signature color.

"That's your family talking, not you. You always follow through for me."

This was true. Where Sue was concerned Chlo was on point. She would back Sue on anything, anytime. How could Chlo ever forget how they had rescued each other that first trying sophomore day?

Chloe had had no one to eat with that first day at lunch and was, like, kinda mortified by the strange phenomenon. Even if you'd never say she was "popular at EP," not that she'd ever strive to be *that,* Chlo always got by. Then, at Roosevelt, it was like she had been shipped off to an even stranger planet than Eden Prep. Besieged with Red Carpetosis to the extreme, she could barely hold a normal conversation without busting out with some random fashion vocal tic which was why she had to escape to the bathroom for a . . . you thought I was gonna say a cig, didn't you? Noo—this was still pre-Marlboro, I mean pre-Dante. There she encountered Sue, in the third stall, all crying hysterically, clutching her hoodie and looking about ready to jump out a window.

"Are you, like, all right?" Chloe had asked.

"Does this look all right to you, china doll?" Sue spat.

"Whoa . . . that was unnecessary. You don't even know me and I was only trying to see if I could help."

"I don't need your help! No one can help! My fucking hoodie is fucked and none of my stupid friends get it. They're like, it's just a stinkin' hoodie, girl—and you know, it's *not* just a stinking hoodie. It's my hoodie, my oldest hoodie, my favorite hoodie, from, like, my dad hoodie! Nobody gets it. Why am I even telling you this?"

She was laughing and crying and Chloe felt compelled to take a look at this fucked-up hoodie situation and try to fix it herself.

"Oh, but I know. A hoodie is *never* just a hoodie. Like, I totally get that." Chloe reluctantly assessed the damage up close. It was kinda severe. The zipper had caught on something and wasn't about to let go either—tiny teeth clutching the cotton fabric with all its life. Chloe maneuvered the pullie back and forth and slowly, like magic, the zipper teeth released. The hoodie was like new. Well, like old-new, and Sue was beside herself, big emerald eyes bulging wide.

"You know," Chlo suggested, "it would actually be kinda dope if we made this hoodie into a capelet—with, like, snaps. We'd keep the original fabric but just change it so you'd never have to deal with a busted zipper again."

Sue was intrigued.

And that was that, two and a half years ago.

"Post-emo might be over," Chloe surmised. "But Dante and I are not, OK. He's familiar and comforting and—hmmm, I guess he's like smoking, something that's bad for me but I like it anyways. And if someone tells me I *have* to do anything you know I won't even if I should. Put it this way, if they were actually good for me then I'd probably have no problem quitting them."

"Que what, Wong?" Sue modeled the parka and admired herself in the mirror.

"Like shopping late at night, Sue, secretly online, or even doing what we're doing now."

Sue groaned. "But why is this bad? Wrong? Everything with you is bad or wrong? Why's it always gotta be like that?"

Chloe was going to respond but then, an oasis in the midst.

"Look, Sue! Gypsies!" She grabbed Sue by her messenger bag and the girls started giggling in excitement. The Gypsies were Chloe's ultimate favorite vendor at the trusty El Conejo Swap Meet, an outdoor sprawling ghetto-fab affair. Sue and she would get these insaaane acrylics and maybe get a hat airbrushed for Dante or find some new baby thermals and then, sometimes, if they were lucky, find the Gypsies.

Today's plan was like this: Procure the goods for Chloe's back-to-school prison look and sew something new for Sue. But first, they'd have to find the Gypsies and buy the following things: a macramé appliqué, gold thread, three yards of black and white handkerchief linen (the really thin transparent kind), and something striped with stretch for her prison-y cap. Then they'd go to the Promenade (all roads somehow ended there) and find basic, cheapy tanks and tennis skirts for Sue to dye and spray-paint. If there was time left they'd go to Baker Hardware for metallic dyes (they had this amazing pewter that glowed), then go back to Sue's and sew.

Chloe originally was supposed to meet Spring at Crystal Court at four but she really had no interest in being in Neiman's-Nordstrom's land where she might run into her mother and get busted. Plus, Spring would probably be with the Wells Park crew led by her all-time nemesis, Crystal Court, who, like, the whole shopping complex was named after. Can you imagine?

Ew.

You might think Chloe would think this was cool, but oh, au contraire. To think that a million people would publicly associate you with the name of *just one* shopping experience, even if it was a supposed luxury complex, would be terrible mass exposure pinning you to a single bogus label you had to wear for life!!

Well, just in her opinion. Which was an opinion she openly voiced way back in eighth grade when the Crystal Court opened its fifty-foot doors, little Crystal herself decked out like a Swarovski princess, cutting the ceremonial white bow while simultaneously blinding the well-wishers with her bedazzled getup. She and Crystal had hated each other forever, well, ever since third grade.

It was like this. One day in morning assembly Chloe noticed that Crystal was really starting to bite her style, like, down to the way she intentionally mismatched her socks. This, initially, was a compliment. But then, the next day, Crystal took it a bit too far and had the nerve to say Chlo was copying her! At which point Chloe called her out on this blatant lie on the handball court (maybe she did get a bit too close with the ball but she wasn't really gonna get physical).

Crystal freaked. She shrieked like the *Texas Chainsaw* murderer was coming after her and then bit *herself* in the leg. Then she told Mrs. Grossman that *Chloe* bit her!

Even though Chlo had pretty good support throughout the class, at home, Chloe, claro que si, was the big fat liar. Charles Sr. promptly pulled his entire account from Schmukla, Schitty, and Schizer, which was blamed on Stan, who in turn told Lucinda, who of course grounded Chloe forever and made her go over and apologize to the entire Court family during brunch at the Shore Club. She even made her wear this totally heinous and wussy Kermit green Peter-Pan-collar dress with white sandals. You know, the Buster Brown kind with rubber soles and brass buckles. Chloe still hates white sandals to this day. And anything with brass.

It was totally wrong and unforgivable and even though Crystal had apparently, like, blacked out on this experience, Chloe would never forget it. Crystal now pretended to actually like Chlo, in part impressed by her stellar Fake ID connections but probably more afraid that one of her "ghetto" friends might kick her ass. Which was altogether possible since Sue had some notorious anger management issues.

So you see, Chloe just had to flake on Spring. Spring would understand. It was just one of those understood things.

But getting back to the Swap Meet, the Gypsies were way out of place in El Conejo which made them an even sweeter find. Their majestic purple booth was draped like a full-on harem tent with rolls of heavy brocade and candy-colored silks piled high on opulent rugs. Chloe had yet to meet the mysterious owner herself, a woman named Agostina DeZahl, self-appointed Queen of these Gypsies. There was a portrait of Agostina sprawled across the Gypsies' billowing tent—a profile view featuring her apparently signature white cashmere snood and a pair of tortoiseshell wraparounds concealing her eyes.

This was a good sign.

After all, the Gypsies were Chloe's most affordable vendor for fabric since shopping sola naturally meant Chloe was on a sorta-budget. (Stan would never support sewing, a "useless, mindless hobby.") To support her habit Chloe sometimes sold discovered treasures on the sly, online. She was, after all, crafty too. But all too often she'd fall hopelessly in love with her find and at the last minute decide to keep the rescued gem all for herself. Even if she would probably never wear a pair of patent leather gauchos or a size 22 floor-length sequined caftan—she might need them one day. One never knew what wardrobe an unexpected life event might call for.

After-school Activities

DO: Pursue after-school activities

DON'T: Actively pursue boyfriends after school

Do you remember Julius—the tiny schmo who'd been carrying La Contessa's chapel-length silk-satin train? Well, he had finally sent for Chlo. And today would be the day, after school at four.

Chloe rang the bell wearing a structured ensemble of black, white, and green. Her black wool dress fell just above her knees, single green grosgrain ribbon demurely wrapped below the bust. Smart but sweet. For the auspicious occasion Chloe chose a round-neck style with slender bracelet sleeves. The sleeves helped feature her chosen accessory, an opera-length strand of alternating jade and pearls (definitely "fancy"), which she preferred to wrap around her wrist three times so she could hold the excess beads in her left palm like a rosary (not that she owned a rosary).

Her white go-go boots, dead stock—la bomba, zipped midcalf over opaque black wool tights. Demure and impressionable but structured and serious too, exactly how she wanted to merchandise herself today. After all, an invitation to see the Countess was no joke. To impress would be impossible, but nevertheless, she had to represent. Of course, she couldn't look tooo sweet or serious. So her white go-go boots were mod and punk with exposed metal zippers up the sides. (Chloe had sewed them in herself all haphazard-like.) Last minute she slanted a tartan butcher boy's cap, just so, to partially conceal her choppy bangs. Overall, Chloe felt very pre-cocktailly and that was the attire, per La Contessa's request:

PRE-Cocktail Attire
4ish
Merci beaucoup

Chloe's footsteps echoed loudly throughout the foyer. *Oh how she just loved the consistent sound of a good heel clickety-clacking away.* This sound was soon replaced by the distinct hiss and coo of the Countess Coco l'Orange stirring deep within.

Julius and some other schmo unlatched two enormous French doors and waved Chloe into what was the most ENORMOUS little parlor ever, a domed room ablaze in fire engine red and bulbous yellow chintz. A giant taxidermy tiger sprung across the doorway—the memorable lens that focused in on La Contessa's grand salon.

The salon was awash in cream and chocolate, a hint of peach or orange here, a dash of white tiger peeking from there. The Countess appeared to be draped in ropes of pearls and pendants that poured into a silky V plunging down her back. Behind three panels of silk, each one embroidered with silver cranes and flying dragons and pagodas floating atop bright lily pads, Chloe instantly recognized the veiled outline of what was apparently the Countess's signature accessory: a long, golden fake cigarette. Holding court in bias-cut crepe de chine, an eye-popping canary gown completely slit up the thigh, she towered over a little schmo on a stool. The mute little man held a mile-high stack of fabrics, which the Countess either nuzzled to her face or tossed to the floor. At present, she was commissioning new peignoirs in luscious silks, buttery chiffons, and paper-thin georgettes.

"Gooood," she considered, running a swath of silk against a cheek.

"Better," she purred, while the little schmo began to sweat but didn't *dare* move or wipe his brow.

"Best!" she cried, erupting in delight. "Finer than a cobweb." Tossing the whole tray in the air like a salad, she spun around twice and collapsed onto a bright satin divan, braided gold and ivory tassels coiled around its feet. The poor man ducked to avoid the flying tray and was now on his haberdasher knees, trying to pick up the pieces.

"And you know, Chloe dahhling," she chortled, "I am only interested in the best! After all," the Countess continued with a sigh, "there is so much talk polluting our world today about what is bad—bad parties, bad collections, bad husbands, ha! Why support anything bad at all? I choose to live in a world of bests—am constantly on the prowl for that which is even better than best!"

She beckoned Chloe near with a bedazzled pinky. Her emphasis on "bad husbands" piqued Chloe's interest for real. How many *bad husbands* had this Countess had? And wasn't she the one rumored to have cast, like, some evil irreversible spell on all six of them?

"Lesson Number One, Chloe: You must always believe there is room for improvement—that it *is* possible to make something better—even the best." She arched a brow and turned to assess Chloe.

School? The Countess had summoned her for class?

With a diaphanous wrap draped across a shoulder, the Countess began to circle Chloe like a cat. The wrap even matched her single gray tendril of hair—you know, the one that curled around her cherubic face and all.

"This little thing, Chloe dahling, came from a type of llama, a baby vicuña. It was once an endangered species but I secured a few precious cloths even then through a Gypsy friend named Agostina DeZahl, the finest purveyor of black-market fashions. I do wish it was shahtoosh, not to be confused with charmeuse, or shantung, which is a heavy but delightful silk from China, the great mother of all things exquisite. But, alas, I have created enough scandal in my life so vicuña shall suffice for today."

Agostina DeZahl? Queen of the El Conejo Swap Meet Gypsies? What a weird coincidence?!

The Countess returned to her divan and sprawled herself out again. "Come here, child, and touch it." Chloe tiptoed close but felt, like, awkward to say the very least.

"Well, go on, dahhling, touch it I say!"

The Countess hurled the gauzy wrap into Chloe's hands and Chloe felt like she had caught something quite scandalous indeed. She let the fine wrap glide through her fingertips, light as a feather. So soft, it put all Chloe's nine cashmere sweaters to shame, vintage Pringle and all.

"Lesson Number Two: Never wear synthetic anything. Nature, my child, will never betray you."

She pulled Chloe down by her side, losing a gold mule in the process. Chloe lifted the shoe, not a mule but a sandal, startled by its beauty.

"You like? That, my dahling, is authentic Ferragamo. Salvatore gave them to my mother herself. They are his 'invisible shoes.' See these tiny bands here? Nylon, disappear onto your skin—life-is-but-a-dream."

This was too much. The Countess had real original Ferragamo shoes! When, like, Ferragamo himself actually made them! Chloe, like, only had a magnet.

"Now stand up please so I can take a good look at you, pretty young thing."

PYT? Chloe gushed, chest concave, clutching wrists and pearls all nervously.

"Well, you can't stand like that and mean it now can you?"

Chloe didn't know what to do or say or how to stand! She felt totally retarded.

"I see." The Countess hummed, jade-framed monocle helping her to appraise.

"Mary meets Marc—Mary Quant, that is. And you do know which Marc I'm talking about, that Jacobs fellow. I do like the little sautoir wrapped round the wrist—rebellious, yesss for sure. An uncut diamond in the rough. Potential to be polished, but still unfinished. Thoughtful, willing, and willful, self-disciplined—sometimes, curious like a kitten, not quite a cat. Simplee deeevine." She leapt up in a single exuberant motion. Chloe once again was, like, taken aback at this fervent but accurate assessment.

"Now tell me, dahling, something about your styyyyle."

Chloe immediately relaxed. That was easy! "Well,

today, Countess, I was going for an Ode to an English Renegade Schoolgirl thing—"

The Countess swelled.

"Yes Yes Yes!" she squealed, tapping her invisible shoes. "ENGLISH RENEGADE SCHOOLGIRL—English Renegade Schoolgirl!" She grabbed Chloe by her wrists and began twirling her fast.

"That is exactly your present style—Chloe the English Renegade Schoolgirl with the perfectly imperfect pedigree. Stay exactly this way—teachable and smart, but daring too and filled with whimsy. It's quite charming and suits you, or rather since you don't strike me as the suit type in the traditional meaning of this word, although a fabulous white tuxedo suit would suit you well a la Bianca . . . Bianca Jagger, that is—anyhow, this, you, your English renegade schoolgirl style, unsuits you, BEST."

Pleased with this evaluation, she collapsed on the divan, clearly fatigued. "You already knew Lesson Number Three."

She did? But what exactly was the lesson? And what was the question?

"Now what shall it be this afternoon? Irish coffee, espresso bean, cherry whip, or all threeee?" Like magic, a mountain of colored ribbons, swatches, and slippers appeared for the Countess's review. She raised one of several strands of opera-length pearls and began chewing on a strand.

"Which do you prefer, little English Renegade Schoolgirl?"

"Which color, Countess?"

"No, dahling, which flavor? Ice cream, of course. I always do ice cream at half past four." The Countess yawned and stretched. Her fingers were, like, a dizzying array of enormous, flat baguettes. Who needed pepper spray when you had diamonds like that?

"I dooo believe that was enough lesson for one day. Time for my treat. A sweet treat."

But it had only been, like, half an hour. Chloe wanted to stay longer. She wanted to learn the difference between chinoiserie and crepe de chine. She wanted to know how to tell if fabric was fine or false. And which was the good silk—shahtoosh or shantung (or was it charmeuse)? What *was* lesson number three? Didn't things come in threes? As if reading her steamrolling mind, the Countess just grinned.

"Please do keep coming back," she purred.

And with that the Countess winked and rolled over on a silky side, waving ta-ta.

I'm With the Band

DO: Dress for the team

DON'T: Dress the team too

Every time Chloe rode the freight elevator with the band she felt part of something important. She'd never admit this aloud but that's how she felt. Like she was this punk-rock cheerleader, an anti-cheerleader who still offered support, but not, like, obviously, *and* she made Dante look good. Like any good girlfriend slash anti-cheerleader she made an extra effort to really look the part: *hot*—but not like she was trying-too-hard-to-be-hot hot. Of course, this effort was maximized in the presence of other dudes. There was nothing a little bit of jealousy couldn't cure was what Sue would say. Unfortunately, Dante wasn't the jealous type—or at least he pretended not to be.

Chloe had planned this outfit well. She wanted to look perfectly unperfect. She tossed a charcoal striped soccer jacket over her shoulder and felt pleased, although spent, with what she was wearing. Feeling stressed made her just *have* to wake up last night at three to rummage through her dad's old sock drawer and "borrow" something new to wear. She had located some old tube socks and a Hanes V-neck T, the really thin, transparent kind. Armed with her trusty scissors, she cut away. Cutting deep into the neck on both sides transformed it into a slouchy, reversible V. She clasped the gathered fabric at her belly button with a jet brooch shaped like a lotus, and in back the cotton folds did quite a lovely drapey thing. Her dad's undershirt was now a saucy reversible number! In an army green cheerleader skirt and fourteen-hole boxing boots, her dad's yellow and white striped tubies poking out, Chloe looked like a cheerleader—a punk-rock cheerleader, that is.

"James is never on time," Dante complained. He was stomping back and forth in heavy creepers and then, he noticed Chlo. "New shirt, right?"

Mission accomplished. Dante ran a hand through Chloe's pleats and kissed her cheek.

"Thaz how it is with all drummers, Dante—can't rely on them for shit cuz they do their own thang," offered Martin, the hairy guitar player. He definitely did his own thang too—in a nutty-crunchy I-love-soy-nuts-and-smoke-alot-of-pot kind of way. Chloe was yet again transfixed by how wrong his wardrobe was. And then, like lightning, she was on the Red Carpet again.

CARPETOSIS DIAGNOSIS:

SUBJECT: The Mourned

FAMILY HISTORY: N/A and too much to print anyhow

STYLE SYMPTOMS: clashing prints, Jesus sandals (not like I have anything against Jesus' style), ancient Gap chambray button-downs, stonewashed Eddie Bauer pants with LOTS of double reverse pleats, and oyveyEWWW—Guido-y metallic shirts with jumbo jivy collars

ALLERGIES: original belts, *clearly* socks, and one-of-a-kind accessories

Hi, me, it's me with today's Red Carpetosis Diagnosis. Subject: The Mourned.

I'll start with Dante. Hands down, he has all the style. He's trying to work with what he's got and it's just not much to work with. Let's diagnose. Look at T.C. I mean, T.C. is lead guitar! Lead guitar needs to look good and he looks contrived at best—like he's aspiring Rat Pack or rockabilly and the band is neither. Like, the other night he was featuring some *Swingers*-esque shiny shirt that was over before that old movie even came out. And today he's trying too hard again—this time in some trying-to-be-Ashton getup with a trucker hat and contrived western button-down and, like, it's not one-of-a-kind, it's from Macy's. James is marginal. Like, at least he's monochromatic in dark denim with nondescript but nonoffensive shoes but he's hidden behind the drum kit so what good is that? After all, who cares about dressing the drummer? You can't even see the drummer! Then there's Paul on bass. Paul thinks Gap chinos are high fashion. He should buy stock in the Gap. Maybe Mitch could help with that? OK, oh god, here's Martin, the fairest of them all: the King Channeler of ex-hair-band cover boys who decided to go "natural" but kept the hair.

It breaks my heart to say it but they just DON'T go *together* let alone match their genre! The pressure can't always be on Dante to look good for everyone all the time, even if he is the front man. Hmmm . . . maybe it's, like, deliberate? Like, maybe Dante doesn't want anyone else to look good next to him lest he pale in comparison? Well, regardless, his boyz just gotta get it together if they ever want to go into rotation on VH1, let alone TRL.

Carpetosis Prognosis: Downhill and Grim. Total Vomitosis.

★ ★ ★

Coming back from the in-depth coverage, Chlo felt ready to pass out. She gasped and blinked twice as her eyes focused on the unfortunate sight of Martin's very hairy toes.

"DON'T!" she blurted. A shaggy head whipped around. "You just DON'T play a show in TEVAs!"

Chlo cupped a hand over her mouth, mortified.

Martin was not amused. "Dante, tell your crazy bitch to shut the fuck up."

Sue jumped up. "What waz that? What did you call her? And whacha tell her to do?"

Oh god. Oh no. She had done it again. She had instigated. A brawl was about to break out and no, not between her boyfriend who was, like, supposed to defend her, but between, like, one-hundred-pound Sue, ready to throw down any sec, and the three-hundred-pound gorilla.

"You heard me," Martin challenged. "Don't get crazy with me too or I just might—"

"Stop it!" Dante shrieked. He grabbed Martin by his collar—oh wait that's right, he doesn't *do collars,* so by, like, the sleeve.

"Let's all be mature here and settle the fuck down. That includes you," he said to Martin, "and you," he ordered Sue.

Martin and Sue backed down.

"Dante, he can't be expected to be taken seriously! You can't be expected to be taken seriously! Tevas, like, undo all street slash rock slash punk credibility you are trying to create let alone keep! Don't you get it? Don't you watch MTV2? Fuse? All right, so maybe videos are never on TV anymore but image still means everything."

"Chlo—stop trippin'. You're cute but . . . you're giving me a headache."

Shaking his shaved head, he crawled out onto the fire escape to join Martin for some "air."

"Fantastic. Now I hurt Dante's feelings." Chloe felt so sick of herself—her vocal tics—her lack of control. Why couldn't she just stop thinking altogether? Or at least not blurt these things out loud! She hadn't wanted to but she just couldn't help it. What was inside her invariably popped out. "Ignore that macho fool Chloe. The boyz always back down."

They sure did—especially in Sue's family, where they often disappeared altogether. "La familia es todo" might have been tattooed across Dante's back, like, sprawled in these ginormous butch Olde English letters, but for real, he wasn't all that committed to the cause.

Nevertheless Dante and Sue could sling insults back and forth like it was no big thing. Their love would always be sealed in blood. No matter what either of them said or did, their "familia" would always welcome them home.

Chloe tried to reclaim Dante's attention one more time. It was no use; he was still on the fire escape pretending not to see her.

part four

Evaluate a Significant Experience, Achievement, Risk You Have Taken, or Ethical Dilemma

[Ethical Dilemma? Hmmm. Chloe's had several.]

Gifts

DO: Accept gifts from strangers

DON'T: Assume all gifts are good

Chloe's cell phone shook all the way across her vanity from one side to the other, knocking down her latest Polaroids. She picked up without checking to see who it was, something she quickly regretted.

"Oh, hey there, Spring."

"Chlo! Where have you been? I've called you like fifty times!"

Fifty-six was more like it.

"I've been over there every day checking on you.

I've been worried sick. Your mom said something about you being on a retreat—like, what's that about?"

"She said that? That just means I'm grounded." Chloe sighed and looked out into the wide hall for any signs of Lucinda life.

"Mitch hasn't mentioned anything weird at all. When I ask about you he just shrugs all nonchalant. SO, like, did you tell them or what? Cuz they didn't seem upset so I'm assuming you didn't?"

"No, Spring, everyone is just being their typical shut-up-and-smile selves. I did tell them everything and kinda got kicked out and it royally sucked. I even considered shlepping to Sue's but was, like, in my favorite gold peeptoes so I only made it across the street. Oh, and that's when I met that neighbor lady—the Countess, the scandalous one, even though I don't think she's scandalous at all, I think she's rad. She has diamonds for days. I wish I could've stayed for her party to check out red carpet arrivals but, like, Pau needed me to buy her Tiger Balm. Then Sue and I went shopping for parkas—oh but if my mom asks I was with you, OK—and we, like, couldn't get to Crystal Court in time to meet you and honestly I didn't wanna see Her Glitterina Highness in the flesh. Plus I've been on FD overload—it's been epic."

"Whoa, wait a sec. That was way too much information to be delivered over the cell. Can I just come over already? You can't still be mad?" Spring held her breath.

"Not a good idea, Spring Bean. Not today. And no,

I'm not mad at you but I gotta feel this not-going-to-college thing out alone. More importantly I gotta figure out how to sneak out of the Tower. Dante's playing and Lucinda knows I've been escaping."

"Can I come?"

"You need an ID, Bean. A good one."

Spring fell silent.

"It's not my policy, Spring. It's California's."

Silence still.

"Look, I'm not gonna play this pouty why-can't-you-get-me-in game right now when I have my entire future collapsing around me!"

"I'm sorry, Chlo. It's just, Sue doesn't have an ID and she always goes."

"Sue slept with the doorman! And that only earns her privileges for so long anyhow. Listen, Spring Bean, I gotta go. By tomorrow, I promise I'll have pre-deb-dress sketches to show you!"

"Promise?"

"Swear."

"All right. I love you."

Chloe grimaced. Why did Spring have to say I love you, like, every five seconds?

"Me too," Chloe managed to reply. With that she flipped her cell shut, just as her door swung open.

Lucinda stood framed by the door, arms folded across her ivory cardigan. She held two Nordstrom bags in one hand, a Williams-Sonoma bag in the other.

"Hi, Mom," Chloe whispered, not knowing what to make of her mom's sudden appearance. Swathed in ivory cashmere, she looked soft, innocent even. Chloe blinked. It must have been a mirage.

"The door was open so I didn't knock."

"That's all right. It is your house."

Lucinda took a grand step forward. "It certainly is. For a girl who strives to dress like she's been in a blender you sure do keep a neat room."

Chloe was confused. Was that supposed to be, like, a compliment?

"These are for you," Lucinda announced, depositing the bags on Chloe's bed.

Chloe was way confused. "Gifts? I don't get it."

"You *should* consider them gifts." Something in Lucinda's tone suggested these, in fact, would not be gifts at all.

"Chloe Wong," she began, "your father and I have taken some time to recover, and yes, discuss your limited options at length. Seeing that you have now missed all deadlines for acceptable state universities, which we had thought were the last resort, AND since you failed to take the SATs altogether, you shall do the following: enlist in city college right after graduation and hope you might one day be accepted into a decent state school. Of course, you will be living here since we will not support or finance any 'plans' that don't include attending a real college, particularly of the fashion variety. If you refuse, should you dare—then behold your only other options."

Lucinda pointed to the bags and stepped back. These were definitely not gifts. *Were they bombs? Would her mom seriously consider blowing her up?*

"What's inside?" Chloe asked reluctantly.

"Open one up and see for yourself."

Chloe gulped. Was it some humiliating Nordstrom Mommy-and-me getup? Could it be Chloe's violated holiday novelty sweater? Did Lucinda chop up her favorite fuchsia pea coat?

Tentatively, Chlo removed three silver boxes from the bags and untied the first gigantic silver and gold bow. She lifted the lid and unfolded the white tissue, feeling something heavy and rigid underneath its perfect folds. It was definitely a uniform. A maid's uniform. Just like Lupe's.

"I don't get it," Chloe uttered while holding a smocked apron high.

"Get this, Chloe Wong. It is what you will in fact be wearing every day for the rest of your life since you think you don't need a college education! Or, if you prefer, you might be wearing what's in here." She pointed at box number two.

"Open it," she demanded. "Now!"

Chloe's stomach dropped. This was certainly cruel and unusual punishment. Her mom was making an example of her. She was attempting to make some vindictive and ridiculous point with costumes—bad ones at that.

Opening box number two, Chloe took out a white blouse and pair of black slacks, the undeniable uniform of a Shore Club valet.

"Did you know they let women park cars now too? Things in this patriarchal world are changing every day!"

I mean, whose battle was this anyhow? Chloe felt angry and afraid and even sorry for her mom. Then Lucinda let out a strange and solitary cackle, pushing the final box forth. Clearly, she had gone mad.

"Last one—open, please."

Chloe was horrified. Out popped a plastic badge revealing her first name, next to the words HI, MY NAME IS.

"I figured you could use your vivid imagination for that one." Lucinda's eyes glazed over, pupils dilating wildly. She began to tap her toes. Yep, black and tan flats. Patent leather. Probably Chanel. She must have owned, like, seventeen pairs.

"What am I supposed to do with these, Mom?" Chloe ventured.

"Why should an aspiring working-class ingrate need nice, upper-class clothes? An uneducated girl has no need for an educated person's wardrobe. She only needs the uniform of the working class, people who live in neighborhoods where they kill each other and steal things, like the neighborhood your friend Sue lives in!"

"Why do you have to put her down too? You've made your point. I'll get a plan. And it won't involve wearing one of these."

Chloe bunched up the apron in a ball and threw it at Lucinda just as a salt-and-pepper beehive peeked into the room. Pau was eavesdropping?

"Mother?" Lucinda queried, turning around. Pau-Pau slowly shuffled into the room and began to pick up all the things strewn across the floor.

"Hi-yaaa, Lucinda. Just like a low-mean pau."

Chloe knew exactly what that meant. It meant an-old-mean-lady. Her grandma had called her mom an old-mean-lady! She didn't know which was more offensive, the old or the mean part.

Lucinda teared up and threw her hands down. "I have to check on your juk, Ma. Juk I made for you!" Like the petulant adult-child she was, she stormed out.

"Thanks, Pau," Chloe whispered. "You saved me again."

"Tut. For long time Pau-Pau wear smock like this."

Pau-Pau smoothed the smocked apron and examined the tiny folds. Chloe felt a wave of guilt but didn't know why. She focused on the tiny folds instead, firmly pressed creases.

"Your ma, Chloe-girl, Pau-Pau like call, mo-dom. You come upstairs. Pau show you how make tickpins."

"You mean pintucks?"

Pau waved the correction aside.

"Maybe later, Pau. I, um, like, have to go to the library." Why did she just lie? She didn't have to lie to Pau.

"It's for a big assignment, on Chinese history actually."

Why'd she, like, lie again? Pau tossed a piece of ginger into her mouth and pulled a bag of Fritos for Chlo out of her robe. Chloe felt even more guilty since Fritos were her *favorite* all-the-time anytime snack.

"Thanks," Chloe whispered, popping open the bag.

"You think pintick hard?" Pau remarked, helping

herself to some chips. "Mo lay yel. Not so bad. You come up later. Pau-Pau show Chloe-girl how."

She zipped her navy velour robe high and walked away, distinct little tat-tat-high slapping.

Chlo felt pathetic: grounded, disowned, and now a compulsive liar too? Lying to her favorite family member no less—the only family member on her side? She had to escape. To quote one of her all-time flashback favorites, Morrissey, when he was still in The Smiths, "What difference does it make?" What difference did it make if she snuck out again? Sneaking out was a big ol' DON'T in theory, but, like, in truth and practice it was the only thing she could DO in the fortressed Wong-Leiberman world.

Red Flags Get Redder

DO: Try to match your fake ID

DON'T: Identify with anything fake

The Red Room was just that, all red. And The Mourned was set to open the night before the rest of the shitty bands that usually made the round on the local downtown scene. Again. Like, they had played the Friday night showcase for two years, convinced there finally would come a night when the "big" A&R guy from whatever record company was gonna show and sign them.

"Sunny Fujimoto. I think that's the best one yet,

Chlo." Sue examined Chloe's fake ID close, but Chloe was fat-munging, again.

"Chlo, hello-o-o. Earth to Wong!"

Chloe was nowhere near Earth. She was seeing red flags pinned to Dante and it was really distracting. You see, whenever Chloe saw a problem of the wardrobe variety walking down the hall a red flag would follow them too—until she literally "corrected" them with a look more to her liking. Sometimes, text messages floated inside the flags—like constantly shifting Internet pop-ups, really unexpected and annoying. Messages could vary at any given moment, from "mall victim" to "label groupie" to "I know I wore this yesterday."

It wasn't like she enjoyed seeing red flags flapping about. Trust me, it kinda sucked. Like, say, now. Dante was doing sound check. He was strutting back and forth onstage, like, more times than necessary, just to preview himself. A gigantic banner-sized red flag was pinned to his deconstructed military button-down and it said "ALL ABOUT ME" (remember, we kinda covered this narcissist thing already).

Chloe was beginning to feel dizzy and claustrophobic in a sea of so much red when suddenly a six-foot Amazon popped into view. Oy. Vey. Ew. It was the Brazilian shopgirl. Siena.

"Forget that puta," muttered Sue.

Forget her? How could she forget someone with that much fake tanner? The girl was like a gigantic orange—but smeared with lip gloss. Not exactly jealous, Chloe was more insulted that Dante used to date a girl like her, someone who considered board shorts and body suits high fashion.

"How can she go out like that? She's at a bar, not the beach!"

Sue laughed. "Que what? Is that all you're thinking about? Her style?"

"More like her lack of."

"All right. Stupid question. But Chlo, he doesn't even like her. He never even did! Who's more insecure—you or him?"

Touché.

"Wong, they're, like, history, OK. I'm just telling it like it is. Just . . . don't think about it." She spat out an olive pit, messily.

Just don't think about it? Chloe's gao-chaw look said it all. Maybe Sue was the kind of person who could say "Just don't think about it" and do exactly that—not think—but Chlo, she was *not* the type of person who could just not think about something and be cool with it, the kind of girl who could just forget that her boyfriend was probably cheating on her with a Brazilian ho-bag, that she had disgraced her family name, *and* that she was still *sans* postgrad plan! At that moment, Chloe felt totally hopeless. She felt nauseous and grossed-out and all alone in the world—crazy and afraid and trapped with her stupid FD. Was she always going to be like this?

"We don't *have* to come every week you know," Sue offered.

"Neither does she. Anyway, then you wouldn't see you-know-who." Chloe tilted her head in the direction of Omar, the burly doorman, who nodded back, winking at Sue.

"Omar? I'm over that fool. Besides, there's this new hottie over at the Fix. Bartender—hel-lo, free drinks? Maybe we should just go there."

Chloe rolled her eyes, sipping a watered-down Coke. Free drinks. That was all Sue ever thought about lately. Chloe hated to drink but definitely needed a cigarette. This meant she needed to go back to Sue's to get her smoking sweatshirt, which, ironically she'd forgotten. Maybe she should just bail. She felt sick and tired of sitting in that crimson booth staring at the puta's bad beachy clothes. Who, FYI, crossed the stage and handed Dante a note, skanky wardrobe coming into center-stage view.

Noooo . . . way. . . . Can't be!

Chloe went ashen. Her jaw dropped right next to the bowl of mixed nuts. The Brazilian Shopgirl Puta was wearing *her* shoes! They were wearing the *same* shoes! Chloe didn't know whether to laugh or pass out. How was that possible? She had bought her shoes in Chinatown three years ago! As in San Francisco Chinatown, not L.A. Chinatown! And even though they were mass-marketed now, no one in the surrounding Wells Park environment even knew where Chinatown was, L.A., S.F., whatever! And here, tonight, right before her eyes, were HER shoes, her pink cotton (NOT mesh) kung-fu slippers with the single white peony embroidered on the toes? On someone else? On the Brazilian Shopgirl Puta Ho-bag?

Things couldn't get worse.

But apparently they just had.

"I—I gotta go, Sue."

Totally discombobulated, Chloe made for the swinging doors. Sue hopped up.

"Hey, wait a sec. What's going on, Chlo?"

"Too much. Look, I gotta get outta here."

"One of your hallucinations? Red flag?"

"Kinda. Listen—I'll see you at school."

"What do I tell Dante?"

"Just tell him . . . something suddenly came up."

She had heard a girl say that on an old TV show once and apparently tonight was her golden opportunity to say it herself. That was it. She was going back to Rosy's to get her smoking sweatshirt, or wait, maybe it was time she . . . went home to work on her fake Saint Martins app?

Thank gawd the coast was clear back up at the Tower. Chloe had mastered the art of sneaking out and, conversely, breaking in. Her house might have been a gated fortress from afar but it was an easy entry once on the roof. She climbed the familiar sycamore, leapt onto the rooftop shingles, tiptoed to the French window wrapped around her room, and was in. Phew.

Chloe landed firmly in her flats and caught a glimpse of herself. Something about her looked different but she couldn't put her finger on it. She decided to Polaroid her entire self: face and all. Why, she couldn't tell you yet. It was a new and strange impulse, for sure.

She added the Polaroid to her latest collage and reviewed. Sure, she had distracted herself at the Swap Meet with Sue, bargained at the Bowl, and sketched sixteen pre-deb dresses for Spring, but she couldn't stop thinking about Dante and Chinese New Year and her mom and those "gifts."

Chloe went into her closet to think. She wistfully admired her neat stacks of Converse, all lined up in a row. She changed into a favorite white pair and lovingly switched the worn laces, storing them in a Lucite box for repairs. She, like, had collected three dozen different laces ever since she learned to tie them in second grade. Yes, second grade. Until then she had no need for ties since she was in love with Velcro. Speaking of Velcro . . . I mean love, why'd she even try so hard? Were she and Dante—oh god, she couldn't say it. Were they . . . done?

Chloe used to imbibe each and every tortured Dante word like some cashmere elixir. Listening to and consoling him felt like she was eternally wrapped in her favorite fuchsia pea coat! In the beginning she could go for days without Polaroiditis. At school, she felt calmer, thought less, and her vocal tics improved a lot, almost going away completely. She wasn't beset with wacky visions or compelled to blurt fashion commentary on the street. She could even sit through dinner and not suffer from Red Carpetosis when Lucinda walked in! Staring into Dante's big amber eyes, totally focused on him, Chloe could forget all about her fashion disorder. Chloe had believed and hoped that in Dante, she had found love. And that in love, her FD might finally be cured.

But, FYI, no human could have relieved her of what was deeply rooted inside and the spell and allure of Dante were starting to fade. Being his besotted Lolita was getting tired and Dante's glossy sheen was getting dull, revealing what Dante truly was, dim-witted. Underneath the obligatory rimless aviators was a self-absorbed, narrow-minded punk, not of the musical variety but of the asshole variety. There was nothing poetic and soft and kind about him at all. And he probably *was* cheating on her with Siena. That was just what he needed, a fawning, fake-tanned aspiring supermodel who didn't talk.

Once upon a time Dante just went well with everything. He worked like a charm, an accessory for all seasons. Or wait a sec, was she, like, *his* accessory for all . . . shows?

Dante and the Dork

DO: Try to relate to good people

DON'T: Stay in relationships just to look good

Surrounded by at least a thousand other under-achievers at Roosevelt High, Chloe Wong-Leiberman felt right at home: average, below the radar, and free to come and go and, most importantly, dress, as she pleased. By 3:03, Roosevelt was a deserted wasteland. Papers, bottles, and abandoned textbooks lay scattered across the cement "yard." Chloe kicked the curb, annoyed. Dante was late. She was jonesing for a cigarette but didn't have her smoking sweatshirt. Plus, if the evil principal, Ms. Luftinker, caught her smoking again on campus that would be her third offense already this year, placing her on "citizen probation" again. Well, that old hag would only have 104 more opportunities to bust her, since there were only that many days left till graduation, if she even made it to graduation.

Chloe rocked back and forth, wishing her slashed peasant skirt could flutter in the breeze, if only there was a breeze, which there wasn't. No coastal breezes here in the sweaty "inland empire"—more the inland armpit, for real. Roosevelt sure was a galaxy far, far away from bucolic Eden Prep, where the light always made pretty patterns on cobblestone paths, seaside temperatures kept everything cool, and the sun was carefully filtered through what were supposed to look like aged and mature trees.

Today, the pavement sizzled. The longer Chlo stared at the throng of exiting seniors the dizzier she became, and now, all together, a stream of clothes, shoes, and accessories collided at once. She blinked to stave off the oncoming inevitable, but it was no use. On a day as bad as this she couldn't help but totally hallucinate.

BOOM! A pair of ratty flip-flops became polished vintage sneaks. POW! A baggy, shapeless sweater was transformed with a fantastic jeweled clasp. WHAM! Dozens of bad logo Ts got fabulously chic—shirred or ruched or turned inside out with exposed zippers and contrasting seams—POOF! Horrendous pleated pants morphed into slim mod trousers. All bad denim be gone! In their place—POOF! Stark white twill, trimmed with back pocket patches or metallic thread . . . As the last Roosevelt kid whisked on by she needed to breathe deep and shut her eyes to make it all stop. *Think of something pleasing, think of something nice, think of never ever having to go to school again!*

Well, that did it. The hallucinations stopped. Ahead, nothing for miles but sizzling concrete. Chloe squinted at the sun and quietly pondered her fate. Would she be grounded just in this life, or in the next three too?? And if she did have to go through the pain and torture of high school again, would she have to wear a uniform as eternal punishment? Or worse, would she be the type of person who'd enjoy it?

By this point she could've walked home, if that was, like, a real option, which it wasn't. Although she *was* wearing old green Cons—beat up to perfection— the only shoes that felt appropriate. They were a senti- mental pair she had kept in her locker ever since seventh grade and they reminded her of softer, easier times when life was much more certain, less complex, and you didn't have to wait around and worry about whether your supposed boyfriend would forget to pick you up.

Then, while staring vacantly into the light, an all- too-familiar shadow suddenly popped into view with nowhere to hide. It was the stalker himself: Peter Albert Windemere the Third.

"Oh, hey, Chloe. What's up?" he asked, trying to act all nonchalant, like this was some spontaneous coinci- dence they ran into each other in the Roosevelt parking lot when he didn't even go to Roosevelt!

Peter had been stalking, or, like, *really* into Chloe since forever. Or, at least, since second grade. For real. During recess he used to bury his face in her hair and beg to smell it.

At least he had the sense not to come and stalk her still in uniform. Peter went to Eden Prep, and an Eden Prepster just might get his Dockers-clad ass kicked hard if he hung around Roosevelt much longer. And what was up with the Frodo footwear? Clogs? Sandals? Sandalclogs? Open-toe shoes like that, on dudes, made her picture leaping furry hobbits. Not exactly the epitome of hotness.

"Peter, why don't you just give up already? I mean, I'm not even nice to you!" Why did guys always seem to like you more when you were mean? Chloe jumped up and clutched her python satchel close, prepared to use it as a weapon if things got out of hand.

Then, unable to control himself, Peter blurted out the unthinkable, even surprising himself.

"Chloe, will you be my date to prom?"

Gao-chaw? (Remember? That means she shot him a look of the you-have-got-to-be-kidding-me variety.)

"Just as friends," he added, quickly stuffing his hands into his chino pockets. "Spring would love it. We could all go in the same limo. It would be really fun."

Quelle chutzpa.

Chloe shook her head and walked away. Like a lost puppy, Peter sniffed the air dreamily and bounded down the parking lot after her. In the distance, the long and sleek hood of Dante's 1968 Charger appeared, roaring up the road. Help was on its way.

"Listen, Peter, it's not even March! Why don't you ask someone who, like, actually wants to go with you?" I mean, how mean did she really have to be?

"Anyhow, you should know by now, I'm not exactly one for school activities particularly of the Eden Prep variety."

Peter had come this far and wasn't about to give up now.

"But it'll be an opportunity to buy a new dress!"

Hmmm. Chloe whipped around. He was a shmendrick for sure but a smart one with a point. Amused at her stalker's moxie and perception, she paused. She actually entertained this strange offer—for like, a second.

But then the Charger rumbled to a halt and Dante honked the horn. He lowered his rimless aviators and stared the Dork down, hard. Peter dug his sandalclogs in the grass but matched Dante's stare, much to Chlo's surprise.

"So maybe I'll call you this weekend after you've thought about it—that is, about what you'd wear. And I mean, I'll wear anything you think I should, Chloe. I mean it. I wanna do this right."

"Peter," Chlo began, "it would behoove you not to act so desperate and strange. But since I'm feeling a bit out of it, not to mention charitable, I might actually consider this unconventional proposition."

Peter lit up like a firefly, ready to take off for the nearest light and knock himself out.

"Well, that's just great, Chlo. So I'll call you, or

you'll call me, or wait, you don't have my number. . . . I'll just see you after school Monday."

"Relax. I'll be in touch." With that, she slipped into Dante's Charger and shut the door.

Chloe nervously fidgeted with the seat belt, an old-fashioned buckle type that had inspired her to make Dante a real belt last summer for his birthday. She had gone into KustomKars to source the buckles and everything—using vintage rubber and all. She even made a really cool accompanying cuff out of an old Charger license plate, a Cali plate too. But that was back when he always opened the door for her. Once upon a time Dante always opened the door.

"Have I been replaced?" Dante asked with a smirk. Chloe rolled her eyes. Didn't Dante realize she was in crisis? That she hadn't applied to a single college? Did he even know what college was?

Chloe turned her thoughts to Saint Martins and proms and dresses and how there was no way she could apply or get in or go to prom and be a fun date for anyone. Better just to design a dress than, like, go for real. She was a freak, after all, and Peter was normal. She wasn't like Crystal Court. And she hated those kinds of things anyhow, formals, meet-and-greets, "young socials," team activities.

Chloe clutched the chrome handle while Dante spun a U and peeled out recklessly, leaving a dark plume of smoke, and Peter Windemere, in his too-cool-for-school wake.

part five

Educational Data

[Just a warning: It's pretty grim.]

Academic Probation

DO: Report the latest

DON'T: Be late with your report

"**Off** with her head!" would have been the imperial decree had Chloe not intercepted her report card. Each day was getting progressively suckier at school—two D's in French, a missed pop quiz in English, a bungled project in PE. (Like, how could they give homework in PE?) Her dad still would barely speak to her, Zeyde plotzed every time she walked in the room (like, in the bad way), Mitchell continued to bask in all the Chloe-sucks glory, and, of course, there was that not-so-teensy matter of Dante and the Brazilian Shopgirl. And now, this sucky report card.

ENGLISH:	B-	(that was cool)
FRENCH:	C	(not so cool)
U.S. HISTORY:	B-	(2 out of 3 . . .)
CHEMISTRY:	C-	(oy vey ew . . .)
ALGEBRA II:	D	(crappers . . .)
PE:	F	(for reall . . . ?!)

COMMENTS: CHLOE DOES NOT LIVE UP TO HER POTENTIAL. WE ARE CONCERNED FOR HER ACADEMIC FUTURE AND THEREFORE MUST PUT HER ON ACADEMIC PROBATION.

Academic probation! Again? That was it. Chloe was definitely not on the right list. She was screwed. Oh wait, that's right—she was screwed already. Ha. Why did it matter what grades she got senior year anyhow? It wasn't like she was going to college. Hmmm. Was there any way to white out the attendance part? She hadn't realized she had missed PE, like, oh wow, *sixteen* times this semester.

Chloe waited outside the school counseling office in a mildewy green velour chair and drew over her pink slip—a series of slips actually, little floaty numbers she knew would be just stunning layered for Spring's pre-deb event dress. So far, all proposals had been dissed (typical I'm-not-gonna-tell-you-what-I-want stuff), and

Chloe was getting really frustrated trying to read Spring's mind. She was on a mission. You could even say she was obsessed. She tried letting this designing-a-deb's-dress thing be a bonding experience. She had to prove to herself and to Spring that she could make her dress perfect. Was it that bad then that she had ditched PE from time to time to go shopping for the appropriate tulle?

"Sahaid Ali, Caitlin Lee, Mandy Duncan, Chloe Wong-Leiberman?" Dr. David, the obese and slovenly school counselor, read the names off a list in his signature slow and lethargic drawl. He was such a shlub. Plus, he totally smelled like McDonald's.

Everyone grunted at once like a slouching, preverbal group of Neanderthals. Some shrugged like this was no big deal, just the yoosh, par for the course, others (including just-too-cool-for-school Chloe) utilized the free time to focus on much more important things like, hello, her real pretend life.

One girl looked like the tundra. Was she dead? She could barely move, her pink slip a crumpled, sweaty ball. The Asian one. Caitlin Lee. Of course. She looked about ready to pee all over herself in those purple elastic-waist pants. Why did the Asian girl always look ready to jump off a bridge after a trip to the school office? It wasn't, like, the end of the world. Chloe had been in this office plenty and knew the drill well. You got a mini lecture, then, like, had to write some dumb-ass essay on what you did wrong and why it was wrong and then the parentals were called but if you lucked out and three o'clock rolled round before he got to you, Dr. David might just forget about you altogether or absentmindedly cross your name off his list. (Public school in Cali meant staff was spread *way* thin and stressed *way* out. Teachers always did random double or triple duty so it was no surprise that Dr. David was the college advisor, IT guy, and, oddly enough, nutrition counselor.)

Chloe witnessed each senior disappear one at a time behind two frosted glass doors, like dumb and mute lambs to the slaughter. And then, Mrs. Witchell, the school secretary, blocked her view. She was drowning in a purple "Save the Whales" sweatshirt with what appeared to be a photo pin of her deceased cat, denim culottes paired with very white aerobic Aerosoles. Chloe zoomed in hard but before she suffered the oncoming inevitable—Dr. David shouted her name. "Chloe Wong-Leiberman!"

Chloe rubbed her temples and followed Dr. David (who, FYI, waddled more than walked—kinda like a brontosaurus) inside. Then he grunted for her to sit. (Kinda like a bronty too. But brontys were herbivores which Dr. David most certainly was not.)

"Chloe Leiberman, is it?" He folded his hands in his lap—all awash in fast-food crumbs.

"Sometimes Wong," Chloe replied.

"Hummm . . . sometimes a lotta things according to my records."

Dr. D rested his flaky elbows on a stack of files and lowered his Coke bottles, all serious and stern. Chloe wondered what it would feel like to be cross-eyed, bald, and sentenced to a lifetime under bad fluorescent lighting. She felt momentarily grateful for everything, FD and all.

"So. Let's talk about college."

POOF! Chloe suddenly went all china doll, mute and glassy-eyed. Her thoughts drifted to the embellishment she needed for Spring's dress. She really needed paillettes.

"Don't you want to go to college?"

Maybe some grosgrain ribbons too? To sew along the hem, like, in contrast colors.

"A girl from your kind of family should be going to college."

She was feeling lime for Spring—stepping the green thing up a notch.

"I hear you're a creative type, real good with that fashion stuff. How about FIDM or Parsons?"

Spring was the right time to bring back green . . . an Ode to Renewal, an Ode to Rebirth, an Ode to Reinvention. . . .

"Heck, there's even that design school in London? Had a cousin's son who went there—what's it called. Central Saint Martins."

Mixed embellishment AND spring greens. The next theme for the closet! It could be, like, an Ode to Salad but not.

"Central Saint Martins is pricey but your folks have money."

He handed her a brochure and Chloe snapped back

to the room, peeved. What. Was. He. Talkingabout?! Weren't they supposed to, like, have had this discussion junior year? As in *last* year?

"Saint Martins is, like, for seriously talented people, Dr. David."

"Well, there's no harm in applying. Your grades are stellar, you're real good in art, and your parents are encouraging this."

They. Were. Not! Whaaat was wrong with him? Was he insane?

"Excuse me, Dr. David, but I obviously missed the deadline."

He scrunched up his eyes. "Lemme see. Nope. These foreign schools take international apps real late. You'll have until April fifteenth for Route B. You're right on track—ahead of track, even, for a junior."

For a junior? Hold the phone. Like, as if they were in some totally bizarre mistaken identity show—Chloe was beginning to realize Dr. David thought she was someone else. But who? He chuckled and stuffed the application into Chloe's hand.

"Thanks, Dr. David," she whispered.

"Of course, Caitlin—"

"But it's Chloe."

"Wait a sec here—" Dr. David scratched his head.

"Jeez Louise—I was looking at Caitlin Lee's profile. See—says right here in this memo. Lee—want-talk-design-schools-foreign."

Caitlin Lee? The comatose Asian one hiding in the book? That's why she was in the office? Her parents wanted *her* to apply to Saint Martins?

Hugely offended by the flagrant mistaken identity, Chloe crossed her arms, supremely annoyed.

"So you're Ms.—"

"Wong-Leiberman—the senior on academic probation!"

"Oh yeees. That's who you are!" Dr. David took off his glasses and looked at Chlo, as hard as it is to imagine, like he was sorry.

"Well then, I'm afraid you'll need to shape up these grades. Art school or not—you can't get in anywhere on academic probation, the reason you're here today, right?"

Chloe shrugged. Wasn't he supposed to be telling her the reason?

"There might still be time to get back on track. Well, ya don't wanna repeat the twelfth grade, do ya?"

Chlo just got the meaning of, like, a rhetorical question.

"You're a smart girl, Chloe. I mean, you're part Asian, right? It says right here in this memo. *Other*— Asian and other stuff. I have every bit of faith that you'll figure out a plan."

F-ig-ure-o-ut-a-pla-n. The words rolled out in way slow slow motion and Chloe's head took off like a balloon. She traced the brown leather piping around her tote and drifted even further away. What if she couldn't find the perfect satin trim for Spring's slip? What if Spring hated the dress? What if she hated the dress but pretended to like it anyhow? She was the type to pretend—sometimes, but only when she thought she might make Chlo feel bad. I mean, she might have to deal with clients who pretend to like her, I mean her designs, one day, right?

"And that's all," Dr. David said, rubbing his watery eyes.

Chloe had no idea what he'd just said.

"Thanks, Dr. David. Um, like, may I please be excused?"

The horrendous fluorescent lighting might just lead to Red Carpetosis. It featured Dr. David's too-tight poly button-down, little yellow pit stains under each arm— a detail that, HELLO, did not need to be featured.

"Yes, Caitlin, I mean Chloe. It is Chloe, right?"

"Yes, sir," Chloe said. She smiled politely, then practically puked out the door. Caitlin Lee? She had been mistaken for that afashionable loser? Why was she applying to Saint Martins? But wait! *April 15? So she hadn't missed the deadline yet?*

This was it. Chloe had to preserve *some* shred of dignity.

She had totally given up on applying to Saint Martins for real, but today, as crazy as it seemed, she just had to step up. She just had to apply. It would have to be a covert operation (duh?), but it was a risk Chlo was willing to take. But who would give her a letter of rec? She, like, didn't know any of her teachers. And, like, what would her parents do to her if they found out she applied? Or worse, what if she actually got in?

The Virtues of Silk

DO: Go down to quirky places

DON'T: Let quirks keep you down

Julius, La Contessa's number-one schmo, had summoned her again! Chlo felt compelled to refeature her wool crepe dress—you know, the little round-neck one a la Mary Quant. The Countess again featured a swaucy bias-cut satin number, tumbling forth and cascading back—a statuesque column of lace and silk which *was* the chosen topic of that day's lesson, silk that is. The Virtues of Everything Silk, to be exact.

"Do youuu know, Chloe dahling, why I just simply adore silk, do you, hmmmm?"

Chlo shook her head and her beret fell off. She was wearing a tiny knit cap to, like, protect her head—this one in soft buttercream.

"Of course you don't know why which is why I ask the question! It is imperative we ask questions all-the-time!"

The Countess's voice boomed throughout the grand salon—like a powerful freight train on its way toward way important places.

"Anyhoo, back to my point and do you know what the point izzz?"

Chloe shook her head again. *Was that a rhetorical question too?*

"Of course you don't know, silly. How could you possibly know the point when there are several! None of which I have even mentioned yet? The point *is*—"

And with this she drew very close—even her diamonds, la infamous rox, they too smelled like jasmine and cherries, her intoxicating signature scent.

"Pure silk, Chloe dahhhling, absorbs everything. Did you know this? It absorbs even *better* than wool?"

She brushed up against Chloe's wool skirt, like, to illustrate some point.

"No, no—I didn't know that actually," Chloe sputtered.

Like, what was her point? Weren't they just discussing her portfolio? The Five Cali Pieces she would submit for her Saint Martins app?

"AND, Chloe, silk keeps one cool in summer while

keeping one warm in winter. How perfectly phenome-
nal and contradictory is that?"

She handed Chloe a giant swath of silk, kinda like a
one-sheet but not.

"AND silk *looks* so delicate and soft and yet, and
YET—it is the strongest natural fabric EVER. You do
recall what I said about nature, don't you, Chloe
dahling? Ah, yes, the glorious natural silkworm—
mysterious, magical little gem really. But did you know
this?"

Chloe shook her head, rapt with attention. So this
was kinda a lecture—but a good one.

"The silkworm, dahling (which is not really a
worm at all but is a moth), spins a tiny cocoon and inside this very cocoon of swollen mystery lives its
thread. Then, this tiny cocoon must be boiled and
steamed—SACRIFICED even, to yield and unravel its
silk. AND did you know this process smells just horrendous? Offensive even? So disgusting you would
never even want to touch it and yet—and YET, it pro-
duces *this*."

She whipped out a finely spun fan and ran it over
Chloe's knee—again, to emphasize her point—which,
like, Chloe was kind of getting but kinda not. Didn't
the Countess want to review her portfolio? Her Five
Cali Pieces?

"Chloe, I digress, forgive me, please. I think of
China and I get all teary-eyed, weak in the knees—
sometimes I miss her so."

"You mean you, like, lived there?" Chlo's eyes went

wide. Like, her own mother had never even been there and she was supposedly Chinese.

"I've dabbled in Asians—I mean Asia. Shanghai, to be exact. That is where I fell in love . . . ," the Countess reflected, "with silk of course."

She winked.

"Now let's see those sketches, dahling—I quite enjoyed last week's looks. What did you call your—"

"Five Cali Pieces!" Chlo exclaimed. "An Ode to West Coast WASPs is Look Number One. That's, like, named after my oldest friend, Spring, who lives next door—to me, not to you—but your rotunda blocks her mom's view. And then there's Punk Rock Chola Princess—like, my ode to my other best friend, Sue, but she's not really a chola, she's sweet. And then Look Number Three is Velour Relief—like, a tribute to my grandparents—they gotta be comfortable, right, but, like, they can be comfortable and look cool—kinda like those palazzo pjs you were featuring the first time I met you and was amaaazed cuz they looked so rad! Oh and then Look Number Four is all about Swashbuckling Sirens and I'm not sure why yet but I'll let you know when I figure it out, and then of course the last look, my final look, will be all about love—and Dante—he's my boyfriend, I think. We're kinda having some issues right now . . . but that's OK. I'll sort it out."

Oh god. She was doing it again! That rambling thing she always did whenever she was close to the Countess. A curious thing occurred every time she sat on the Countess's little tufted cushion, enveloped in softness and warmth, jasmine-cherry scent wafting above and around. Like, she couldn't stop talking. (But not in an FD vocal tic kinda way—like, she talked about things she really wanted to say.)

She even made sense. Well, in her own quirky way. *Quirky.* That was the adjective the Countess had used to describe her the other week. *"Chloe, dahling, you are positively quirky—just full of splendid little quirks!"*

And a quirk, you probably already know, is a peculiar habit or mannerism, something that apparently didn't bother the Countess at all. You might not know, however, that the word "quirk" also means—in fact its number one meaning is this: a strange and unexpected turn of events. Something Chloe considered now.

"Oh, yes, that Beckett woman. She doesn't care too much for my rotunda, does she? And I thought red complemented her garden—really." The Countess raised her signature fake golden cigarette to her lips and languidly puffed away.

"Oh, but she's lame, Countess. She's just crazy jealous of you cuz you're rad and you've gotten so much attention without even doing anything or wanting it at all. But, like, that's been really inspiring, you know—like, to witness. Someone who does things differently here. Someone who's not afraid to be who they are. I think it's rad—red rotunda and all." God, she did it again!! She used the word "rad," like, twice in one paragraph!

The Countess waved the compliment aside with her gem-encrusted cylinder and rolled over on a hip.

"I DO believe I DON'T have any more time for lessons today. Show me the portfolio when you are done, young quirky thing—I DO look forward to our little meetings so. . . ."

Chloe blushed. Like, hel-lo. . . . She loved coming to the Villa almost as much as . . . the El Conejo Swap Meet? The Promenade? The Bowl? Huh. . . . Like, she secretly wanted to move in! Couldn't the Countess just hide her in a corner somewhere—a little alcove? A closet even? She liked closets! The Countess probably had really grand closets with plenty of space. Surely there was one big enough for her? Maybe she and the Countess could come to some mutual agreement? Maybe she could pay rent somehow—fetch her swatches or ice cream—let Julius take the day off every so often and hang by her side. Oh jeez—oh wait—she was sounding so desperate, so transfixed, so under a crazy spell of fawning adoration—

Ew.

She felt like a stalker.

That wasn't cool.

Chloe skipped down the marble steps in her white go-go boots, extra loud, lapping up each and every single Contessa word like a . . . piece of silk? Didn't she say silk was way absorbent?

Hum. Maybe Chloe understood the meaning of the message after all.

Close Encounters of the Lucinda Kind

DO: Be true to people you love

DON'T: Say you love them if it's not true

Lucinda was home early from Ikebana. Lately, it was all about Ikebana. You know, the strange but beautiful art of Japanese flower arranging that was even featured in that *Lost in Translation* movie. It was kinda progressive for Lucinda. Maybe it was even therapeutic. Lucinda definitely needed therapy. She was exhibiting many signs of post-traumatic stress. Like, she had upped her Pilates classes to compensate for the added mimosas she was imbibing over brunches at the Shore

Club—a response to being forced to digest the word over who got in early to college where—news that sent her into a shopping frenzy, her kind of cardiac arrest.

Today, Chloe felt just like juk. You know, the crazy soup with assorted gross stuff in it. Her head throbbed from all that Red Carpetosis and Wheel of Fashion and the entire day was spent in total FD. It felt like watching every single crappy music-video fashion faux pas EVER! Like, where all the extras converge in "da club" in one overwhelming, mixed-up throng of the worst hoochie-fashions and everyone is so not going together and you alone MUST wade through it all and make it all look right. You *must* fix EVERYONE! She couldn't take it. It was like channel-surfing in her head without control of the remote.

Should she take her chances? Be bold? Drop the latest bomb in one sudden assault then run for cover? What were the chances of making it past Lucinda without saying anything about academic probation?

After all, Dr. David spaced and forgot to call. But then again if he remembered to call he might suggest applying to Saint Martins too. And he was the one who brought it up. If Chloe didn't say anything period then maybe it would be like this whole sucky-grades-and-probation situation never happened at all! Hear no evil, see no evil, speak no evil—the family code, right?

"Chloe Wong, hand me those Brazil nuts please." POOF! Chloe stood face to face with the Enemy herself. Hmm. But the Enemy was talking to her. Was it a trap?

Tentatively, Chloe handed Lucinda a teak bowl.

Lucinda was preparing Wally's special meal—something mushy made from "live" Brazil nuts and acorns. (Now that they were over Atkins/South Beach they were on to "live" and "raw" foods only.) As Lucinda chopped and diced with precision Chloe prepared to break the latest, searching for the right words. But what she ended up saying was so un-right.

"Pleats make you look fat!" she blurted, quickly cupping a hand over her mouth, shocked at her lack of impulse control.

Lucinda went ashen. Chloe kicked herself in the shin.

"They do?" she cried. She began smoothing the creases over what, minus the gigantic pleats, were really un-lumpy hips.

"Pleats like that add ten pounds, Mom. Or in your case, fifteen."

Omigod, Chloe! Stop it already and control yourself! You DON'T comment on your mom's fattening pants when you're about to tell her you're on academic probation, just *have* to go to fashion school in London, and might not even graduate!

But it was no use. It was too late. In moments like these it was as if a force greater than herself pried her lips wide open again and again, forcing insults to keep spontaneously popping out.

"So do I really look fat? You think I am fat. That's it. I am officially a fat Chinese lady." Lucinda sank down upon a bench, on the verge of something, cradling a calico pillow to her chest. Wally waddled over to support.

"Mom, you're not fat at all. I said pleats like that make one, as in anyone, skinny or fat, LOOK fat. This doesn't mean you *are* fat. You're nowhere near fat, for real!"

Chlo bit her lip and then—

"But those pants do makeyoulook fat." Omigod! *She couldn't stop it*. Once it had started, like—her mouth took on a life of its own.

"This low-carb-raw-food plan just isn't working," Lucinda lamented. Wally moaned and rolled to a side, either because he agreed or because he was experiencing some serious post-binge heartburn.

"Why don't you try quinoa, Mom? Mrs. Arriza says it's, like, almost a protein."

This, Chloe thought, was a helpful way to try to make peace. Mrs. A cooked red quinoa all the time and it was really good—in a nutty, I'm-supposed-to-taste-healthy-but-that's-OK kinda way.

"Does Mrs. Arriza think you should wear clothes like *that* in public?" Lucinda challenged, clearly not pleased with the tip.

"I mean would it really kill you, Chloe, just once, just *one* time, to wear something . . ."

Chloe braced herself.

". . . like Spring!"

Like Spring!?!

"Since when did Spring Beckett become the style maven?"

Spring had several endearing traits but she was not the authority on style. Like, style required imagination which is exactly why Chloe was designing Spring's pre-deb-event dress, thank you very much!

"Spring, Chloe Wong, represents Eden Prep well."

"But I don't even go there anymore!"

"Don't," she began, arm raised to deflect the imaginary paparazzi, "remind me. Plenty of girls, Chloe Wong, would give their right arm to attend Eden Prep, to live in a beautiful community like ours, to lead the life you choose to spit upon! Your problem is you are spoiled and just have no idea how privileged you are."

All right. So this might be kinda true. But wasn't her mom spoiled too? And anyhow that wasn't exactly the problem she was thinking of sharing today. . . .

And then, from the corner of her eye, she saw the side door swing shut. Mitchell waltzed in—gym bag casually slung across his broad shoulders, an Eden Prep Lacoste cardigan tied loosely around his neck. For real, Mitchell looked like a walking advertisement for the place, an aspiring demagogue, coiffed to perfection and about to tell you why he's so much better at lacrosse than you'll ever be so don't even bother trying to get on his team.

"Chloe suffers from a highly unusual but fortunately noncontagious disease. I like to call it please-feel-sorry-for-me-cuz-I-don't-live-in-the-ghetto-with-my-ghetto-friends disorder."

"Fuck off, Tucker." Chloe threw a napkin ring at her annoying little brother.

"That's a compliment." He snickered, ducking as the napkin ring fell into the raw soup situation.

"Chloe Wong!" Lucinda cried. "Your childish antics amaze me. Really, they do. Why can't you just follow your brother's lead and try to act mature?"

Mature? Mitch? How could they all be fooled by the bow tie and blazer? Mitchell was an emotionally stunted coward! An overindulged brat! A complete and utter traitor to the cause! And he was only fourteen months younger than Chloe anyhow so to act as if he was some epitome of maturity at, like, six, was total MISREPRESENTATION.

Politically, Mitch leaned as far right as you could go without falling (which went contrary to the original Wong-Leiberman way even if it pleased his Eden Prep peers and their benefactors well). Over the years he had managed to amass loyal followers of both sexes of all ages everywhere—at school, at the Shore Club, at the local banks even, where tellers greeted him by first name! And then there were the ladies—like, he made them all drool.

Chloe wouldn't be surprised if he secretly financed his portfolio by doubling as a male escort for the neighborhood lunch-then-yogilates set, like, during holiday breaks or really late at night. She had tried, honest, to be open to her brother's potential assets if not merits but then his stupid bow tie would remind her of the Brooks Brothers fiasco and she couldn't see anything else.

"In other news, Mom, I got straight A's, again."

Of course. He handed Lucinda a twenty-page report

card with color-coded charts and graphs and everything while she cooed and oohed and aahed.

"Well, well, well. That is just splendid, darling."

Chloe rescrunched her sleeves to endure the inevitable.

"Behold: a bold departure from the honors assignment, but Professor Jecker is thanking me for the stock
tips already." He whipped forth a glossy brochure from
his cordovan briefcase. It read, in a bold font, "The
Gunthrup Value Fund."

"It's outperformed every other fund in its peer
group. We should buy now while it's still below the
radar."

"Oh, Mitchell, dear. You make me so proud, really."
For real.

Lucinda grabbed the thick brochure like a prized
pair of Tod's at an after-Christmas Neiman's sale, transfixed. Nothing pleased her more than to see her favorite child take to the stock market like a fish to the
sea. It was like through Mitch's glory, Lucinda could
vicariously live out her Master, or rather, Mistress of
the Universe fantasy.

"And don't forget rich," he muttered. For *just* a
teensy second, Mitch blushed at the indulgent
comment.

Like, what went wrong? And furthermore, why
could Mitch do no wrong—even when he tried?
Granted he was varsity everything, definitely Harvard
bound like Stan, and always in Eden Prep uniform, but
was that any excuse for Chlo's mom and dad to let him

be such an emerging, gluttonous, capitalist pig? For all his multifarious accolades, financial coups, and winning luck with the Wells Park ladies, Chloe knew the truth about Mitch. One day the rest of the world would see what only she saw, revealing the tiny emperor he really was, sans bow tie and all.

But it wasn't always like that.

Once upon a time, way before Eden Prep and that ill-fated trip to the Promenade Brooks Brothers, Mitchell, like, was normal. He was even, dare I say, fun. Chloe and Mitch weren't, like, BFF—but, they hung out. Especially at Pau's, when she still lived in Great-auntie Li's three-story Victorian in San Marino (that's almost L.A.). They entertained each other lots and laughed all the time with, like, games. There was this one game in particular, their most favorite game of all, and it was called Gypsy.

Gypsy was like this.

Chlo got to be the pirate queen who dressed Mitch, the Gypsy slave, in whatever she wanted him to wear. They'd only play this game at Pau's, and in her closet— well, in Auntie Li's closet since that was the place with the better accessories. (Lucinda would *freak* if they ever tried this at home.) They'd play Gypsy for hours, even coming up with some really fashion-forward looks. Together they'd break into hysterics while draping piles and piles of ridiculous women's clothing on each other like costumes. Chloe sometimes designed full-on outfits for little seven-year-old Mitch. Seriously. Then one day Lucinda caught them in a precarious state of dress and their free-spirit Gypsy days were o-v-e-r.

"Wha-at are you doing in your auntie's closet?" she boomed, her shadow spilling across the powder blue wall.

"And furthermore—whyyy is Mitchell wearing your grandmother's clothes?!!"

Chloe and Mitch hovered in a corner, not knowing what to do.

"She made me, Mom!" Mitch accused. "It's all her fault I'm dressed this way."

Chlo's jaw fell to the floor.

"Ut-uh!" she protested. "You wanted me to dress you like that, you retard!"

"Don't call your brother a retard when he's the one who got A's on his report card last year, missy!"

Shamed and silenced, Chloe gave up. Lucinda grabbed Mitch's tiny hand but before he could go Chloe needed to correct one last thing—the bow tie she had just finished tying on his little chubby neck.

"It was crooked. Now it's straight."

Mitch couldn't look her in the eye then and he hasn't looked her in the eye since. Like, in that one moment he chose Lucinda over Chlo—and he did it again and again and it has been like that ever since. So, to rub salt into the proverbial wound—or, like, to add schmaltz to the stain, the day they were about to be sent to Eden Prep together, as, like, hesitant allies, not like full-on foes (since the five-year interim did give them *some* space to heal)—well, it was like this.

You had two options: to bow tie or to regular tie. Mitch elected to bow tie and Chlo was like, How could you? And he was like, How could I what? And she was like, You know I hate bow ties—like, you know what they remind me of. And he was like, I have no idea what you're talking about. And she was like, Stop pretending, Mitchell, I'm serious. And he was like, Shut up, Chlo, I'm serious too—give me that bow tie. And then Chlo grabbed the bow tie from Mitch and ran out of the store and the Brooks Brothers manager came running after her calling "Security! Security!" and, like, she was accused of shoplifting a dumb-ass Brooks Brothers polka-dot bow tie! And, like, of course, *that* was a scandal that made the Eden Prep wires before she, like, even ever stepped foot on that circular, sun-kissed drive.

And it was like that.

What it was like now was observing a six-foot tan and navy peacock enjoying his reign from the kitchen throne.

"Feel free to peruse the accompanying prospectus while I get dressed for the Club's benefit."

Safe as usual, Mitch disappeared up the kitchen stairs as smoothly as he had slithered on in.

If only Mitch would die. OK, or at least have a near fatal accident that rendered him limbless—speechless—drooling even would suffice! Chloe sank farther down on her stool, mortified by his shameless pitch. Then she reminded herself that her gauzy skirt wrinkled easily and, on autopilot, sat up straight.

"Chloe Wong, either you will dress appropriately

for the firm's benefit too or you will stay home with your zeyde and pau. Naturally, you are still grounded and will not be going anywhere without my approval."

Lucinda marched off and Chloe collapsed on her barstool all alone at that kitchen island—her report card a crumpled, sweaty ball now bleeding pink into her palms, kinda like Caitlin Lee's.

"What's wrong with me? I didn't even tell her about my suck-ass report card let alone my plan!"

Something felt terribly, irrevocably wrong for sure. Chloe felt like how your feet feel after navigating the streets in heels when you really should have worn flats. Swollen, raw, painful—longing for something more comfortable, like cushy sneaks, but totally unwilling to, like, admit to the pain and change! Committed to suffering for the cause—I mean the shoes.

Instead of telling her mom what mattered, like hi this was an even bigger crisis than her not-applying-to-college crisis, she had annoyed her and looked bad in front of kiss-ass Mitch. And she had insulted her by saying she was wearing fattening pants.

Chloe hopped off the barstool and locked eyes with Pau. Chloe, and obviously everyone else, had totally forgotten she was sitting in the breakfast nook this whole time. Chlo watched Pau polish off another bowl of ice cream, part of her hidden stash. The woman had balls, and stealth. Lucinda would freak if she caught her mom breaking the cardinal no-sugar, no-lactose DON'T. Pau raised a tiny finger to her lips and grinned. Their secrets would be safe with each other for now.

part six

Academic Interests, Volunteer Work, Personal Perspectives, and Life Experiences

[Chloe had lots of interests, volunteered plenty (at least, like, her opinions), and had unique perspectives (hello, her FD) and a decent amount of life experience. They just weren't . . . well, "academic." But shouldn't they still count?]

Spring's a Deb

DO: Trust spring will return to Wells Park

DON'T: Return to Wells Park next spring

Ah, the first rites of spring—a welcome respite from the bitter snow and cold, a promise that life will start anew, a time for the debs to come out to the world.

OK, so in Southern Cali the only real part of this change-o'-the-seasons was the deb-coming-out part. Like, every month looked the same in Wells Park, spring or not. It sure looked the same tonight way up on the Shore Club rooftop deck—a perfectly raked stretch of sand spreading forth, fluorescent sun melting into the golden sea. Tables of near-identically dressed nuclear fams sat sipping sunset cocktails or virgin daiquiris—eating popcorn shrimp and Thai chicken satay, Brie-en-filo and tiny tuna rolls. Tonight was the night to celebrate Spring Beckett's about-to-come-out ball, slated for the following Saturday night at the Ritz. This was a big deal and all for any deb, especially Spring. And yet another thing for Lucinda to rue when she admired photos of Spring's billowy marshmallow gown—something very Gunne Sax a la 1988 or Jessica McClintock 19–every year (same thing, different designer)—and a style that proudly hadn't changed for, like, a century.

Chloe had felt honored when Spring asked her to design the special pre-deb-event dress but she almost cried when Spring asked her to style her too! That, like, required serious trust. Chloe realized this night would mark important history for Spring and even if she and Spring had less and less in common they still shared history which was an important thing to share, even, dare I say, celebrate.

Spring looked just like a frothy lime soda in tea-length tulle, her wavy locks threaded through a rhinestone tiara. Even though Chloe knew she had to work within definite deb parameters like DO work with duchesse satin and DON'T expose toes, Spring really let Chloe step it up a notch by allowing her to introduce both a new pattern and a bold accessory. The confirmed look was altogether acceptable for Chloe, a refreshing variation on West Coast WASP. Cute and conservative, but also fun and free.

Spring flitted about, greeting well-wishers with a polite nod and kiss, her satin slingbacks playfully slapping the ballroom floor. The shoes, thank gawd, were not dyed to match, a coup for Chlo, a leap for Spring, an upset for her mom. Instead, they were a contrasting tulip pink and they complemented her little vintage polka-dot clutch, a really cool find in Mrs. Beckett's "Goodwill" closet. That old thing? Just like Lucinda, Mrs. Beckett belittled all things vintage, preferring things to be brand-spankin'-new—excluding scandalized divorcée neighbors, of course.

The Eden Prepsters arrived in appropriate droves, waltzing back and forth in sweater sets and khaki suits, fruity shifts and silk capris. Chloe could really go Red-Carpetosis-crazy watching alternately well-fed and well-starved bodies feature a predictable array of "classics." She hightailed it to the other side of the deck, shielding her eyes from the view. Being at the Shore Club ALONE (as in sans Dante) and UNARMED (as in dressed "appropriately") was tricky for sure, definite slippery ground.

Chloe had dressed "appropriately" out of respect for Spring, semi-appropriately that is—like, an Ode to Classics with a Chloe Twist. Her chosen Lilly Pulitzer dress was vintage, a compromise, but she refuse-refused to wear a headband even though it could've been kitschy and cute. Instead, she put her hair up in a high-knotted ponytail, with fuchsia chopsticks poking out haphazardly. Then she needed some noise, claro, so she added an elbow-length stack of lime bangles with crazy charms.

Chloe hesitantly craned her neck to look out for a sign of friendly life but was blinded fast by a Red Flag, a bedazzled one, and its name was Crystal Court.

"Chlo-e Leiberman? Omigod? It is you!"

Flanked by: Peter Windemere (like, did they get back together?), the skeevy Logan girls (ew), and Mitchell (quelle surprise); Chloe couldn't decide who to correct first. Unfortunately, Crystal actually had style—not Chloe's style but Crystal style which meant Chloe couldn't correct anything since it was for real (the style part).

"What's up, Crystal?" Chloe tried being "cordial." Plus, she could appreciate the sexy-preppy thing Crystal had going on. A pink and green strapless Lilly number—lemon cashmere cardigan with star-shaped Swarovski buttons tossed around her shoulders, a chunky pearl cuff (hmm—forward for her) worn with closed-toe pointy heels and a yellow satin clutch— Kate Spade? Coach? She couldn't tell but it worked. Touché . . .

"The yoosh—prepping for SC with the girls. It's so exciting! Where-are-you-going-to-college?"

Crystal spelled this last part out, like, in twisted sign language, her type of joke. The Logan girls snickered. Mitchell skulked away. No doubt the association with his non-college-attending sister was bad PR. He had some schmoozing to attend to over by the bar for the investment club anyhow.

"I'm actually not a fan of colleges, Crystal. It-goes-against-my-cult."

The girls guffawed unilaterally. For real, they guffawed. (You know, like the sound of really manic caged birds? Well, that was the sound.)

"Real-ly, you don't say? What cult is that?" Crystal asked.

"Oh, I was just initiated. It's a cult for people who are allergic to school. Sometimes we even make sacrifices late at night for, like, our gods."

The guffaws stopped. Suddenly, Crystal looked confused.

"Is that, like, a real Lilly dress?" she huffed, eyes bulging wide.

"Uh-huh, like, it is," Chloe replied.

"Hmm. So is mine. But yours looks old."

"Chlo's dress is vintage, there's a difference," Peter interjected.

That was bold. Peter didn't have to like—defend her?

"That means it's unique."

But he just did.

"Unlike some, Chloe wouldn't risk attending a crucial event like this in a dress that someone else could've bought, or maybe seen her buy, then decided to wear. As in, copied. That just might be grounds for murder—in her aforementioned cult."

So he was on her side after all!

"Hmm. That's alternative, Chloe," said Crystal. "Well, it's refreshing to see you at least take a fashion cue from the right people. We were starting to worry about you."

"Thanks for your concern," Chloe deadpanned.

"Well, ever since you were 'asked to leave' Eden Prep people can't stop talking about the colorful company you keep and the, like, shady road it's taking you down. I mean, considering you're not even going to college."

Chloe just might have had to do some serious re-enactment on the psychodrama therapy tip and bite Crystal after all.

"Crystal, it must suck being you—being, like, bitter and jealous and always in a cardigan."

Crystal shifted in her little kitten heels and laughed. "Excuse me? Jealous of you? You're kidding me, right?"

"You've always taken pride in being a third-generation Eden Prep girl—someone who's really educated. We even petitioned together for Intro to Psych. Remember? Ninth grade? People only talk shit about other people when they secretly deep down inside can't stand who they are—and sometimes, maybe in this case, might even want to be like the person they're talking shit about. So that must be it. You must wish you were like me. Or maybe, Crystal, deep down inside—if, like, that was actually a place you could go—you just wanna . . . hook up with me?" Chloe added that last part just to really freak her out.

Which it did. Crystal gasped and recoiled.

"Nothing's changed, Chloe Leiberman, since you bit me in third grade! You have no class."

She stormed off now, little court in tow. Peter stayed behind.

"You know, threatening to get physical with her gets her good," he said.

Chloe inhaled deep. "Crystal is quite afraid of confrontation. But then again, sometimes so am I."

She lit a cigarette, sans smoking sweatshirt. Peter looked all concerned.

"And please don't tell me I shouldn't light up right now, Peter, cuz I already know I'm not wearing my smoking sweatshirt."

Peter smiled.

"Actually, I was gonna tell you I think you look extra . . . hot tonight, Chloe."

He blushed. She blushed. Chloe took a long, embarrassed drag.

"Oh," she muttered, looking down, then honing in on Peter's—oh jeez, Bass loafers? Like, why? Chloe just couldn't help but comment.

"Peter, have you ever thought about getting, like, different shoes? Maybe one day we can go shopping and I'll make some suggestions." Wow, she was actually being nice. Wait a sec—who opened her mouth and offered to hang out with Peter? Peter Windemere, as in, the Stalker?

To her pink surprise Peter didn't respond like a stalker freak.

"When some time frees up. I know you got important things to finish, Chloe."

Then they locked eyes, just for a sec. Peter had really nice eyes. They changed color depending on his mood. OK, so he had nebbish style but, for real, he was kinda a mensh.

Huh.

Should she go to prom with Peter? That would make her folks pleased and she certainly could use some extra credit there. It would cause a brouhaha at EP, no doubt, but it also would make it up to Spring, who had felt left out of her world forever. And, of course, it would make Crystal seethe and topple over in her Kate Spade kitten heels! It would be just as friends, of course, and she needed a . . . friend. She certainly needed perspective in the male department. He was, after all, jeez, nice. She couldn't remember a single time when Peter hadn't let her go first or she had sneezed and he had forgotten to say "bless you," even way back in second grade. Oh, and FYI, he always remembered to open doors.

25% Buttahfat

DO: Chew the fat

DON'T: Butter up

"Today's looker, Chloe, is tomorrow's buyer. Come here and admire this dress. See the buttonholes, HAND sewn. Alas, such workmanship today is so rare it's a pity. But there will always be that discriminating eye who needs to have something rare indeed; in fact that person will simply die if he or she goes without!"

All worked up, the Countess flung off her robe, an elaborate floor-sweeping number embroidered with tigers and lilies and pagodas and palms. Reclining in a signature silk-satin gown clinging to EVERYTHING, the Countess looked like a cool drink of lemonade. Yellow, she said, was her signature color—a color she encouraged Chloe to freely embrace.

"But Countess, don't you ever feel, well, guilty for having so much stuff?" The Countess was certainly decked out with major stuff today. La Rox, dozens of them, sparkled from her fingers and wrists and, of course, her infamous décolletage.

Chloe felt like questioning everything. She stood at ease in her signature Mary Quant–ish dress, her chosen uniform for these after-school tête-à-têtes, lessons of the garden fashion-school variety. It wasn't like the Countess told her she had to wear a uniform or anything fancy or that—she just felt respectful dressed this way. Dare I say, appropriate.

Chloe was summoned by Julius for "pre-cocktail" hour twice a week at four. She and the Countess convened in the Grand Dressing Salon which was just that—an entire suite of grand rooms devoted to even grander dressing. Chloe hadn't yet gained access into its candlelit recesses but she imagined it was all giant gilded mirrors, dramatically lit platforms, and cushy luscious couches for the Countess to lounge and loll upon as the minions tended to one of her many fittings, or fits.

Spellbound, Chloe would listen to the Countess recount her days in Paris as a coveted client of the haute couturiers, her stint as a designer in London, or her short career as a buyer in N.Y., the tales always interlaced with scandal or danger and romance, each adventure and affair complete with an accompanying wardrobe that followed her across whole continents.

The Countess often ordered fur-lined slippers or satin mules, a custom tiara or afternoon hat. Chloe got to sample and even offer her opinion on the deluxe goods about to be made. Then, sometimes, they just sat and ate bowl after bowl of ice cream while Chloe showed the Countess the latest from her growing portfolio—which was growing into something much bigger than the five original Cali pieces she planned to submit to Saint Martins.

"Guilt, Chloe, is a waste of my time and yours. Guilt serves no one, ever." Waving the fake golden cigarette in the air indicated she was about to launch into another major lecture. (But a good lecture, mind you, not the when-Mom-reams-you-a-new-one kind.) Chloe perched on her little tufted chair and took perfect mental notes.

"I serve beauty, Chloe. That is my life's path and in that, there is no shame." She spooned another helping of ice cream, something cherry red, and dreamily licked the spoon.

Today, the Grand Salon had been transformed into a full-on ice cream parlor! A harem of confectioners appeared at La Contessa's side, replete with old-fashioned creamers, tall bottles of syrups, and fancy demitasse sets. Heavy ornate trays appeared like magic, held up by miscellaneous schmos who offered Chloe tiny round cups and itty-bitty spoons.

"Twenty-five percent butterfat!" the Countess exclaimed. "Now that, Chloe dahling, is the real thing." Coiled up like a satin ball, playfully dangling her slippered feet, the Countess was in ice cream heaven. A for-real butterfat reverie.

"But Contessa, like, don't you think the pursuit of clothes is, well, sometimes lame?" Chloe stared at a mile-high stack of chunky fur and heavy cashmere, now discarded by her side. The Countess already had ordered coats for fall and was now commissioning lighter peignoirs for "resort and holiday," as in the winter "holiday" she planned to take along the coast of some faraway sea.

"Chloe, dahling, you are too young to be saddled with such guilty thoughts. Guilty guilty guilty, it's enough to depress me so! You are nubile, fresh, and new. Let your mind and body be the same! You have an eye and that eye is a gift! You may even have the all-seeing eye but since you are young you think that this eye will trick you—that it is bad, always wrong, that it sees too much. You judge it and call it trite, or rather what is that word you use . . ."

"Rad? I mean, lame?" Chlo offered.

"LAME! That's the word and this is not so. This eye of yours is like magic. It is your window into a world so beautiful, so unique, soo filled with endless wonder you can't possibly begin to seeee. Your quest for the best will be a noble one indeed."

"So then making clothes can be noble?" Chloe proposed.

"Why yes, because creation is noble!" The Countess tossed a spoon to the ground. It made a lovely pinging noise on the tile.

"Chloe, alas, I do not have this talent. I have the talent for seeinnng talent in others. And, as I just said, I celebrate creation because it is noble. In fact, I celebrate it all!"

Chlo sat up straighter now, nodding emphatically.

"Julius!" the Countess snapped. "Bring my little schoolgirl her letter."

A letter? Julius emerged from the shadows carrying yet another tray. Upon this was a sealed envelope addressed to Central Saint Martins, stamped with La Contessa's wax seal.

Chloe lit up and dropped to her knees. "You wrote me a letter of rec! Omigod, Countess, thank you so much!"

"Pish-posh. It's just a little letter."

"No, it's not. I could just cry! Or die! Really—you have no idea how grateful I—"

"Stop groveling, child, or you'll wrinkle that Mary Quant dress! Anyhow, I love letters, especially when they are about cute, nubile things like yourself . . . so delightfully odd."

Chloe blushed.

"But no time for any more lessons today. Je suis fatiguée—all that boasting about you has rendered me quite exhausted."

"I totally understand, Countess. I'm honored and flattered. God, no one's ever recommended me for anything!"

The Countess waved her off, but a mere trifle, and

returned to a new tray of bonbons, this one placed next to a plate of gilded feathers.

"I'll let you get back to your sampling. Thank you, Countess. Thanks, Julius. Thank you so much!" Cradling the letter close, Chloe curtsied and skipped out into the marble foyer, Mary Jane heels loudly clickety-clacking down the hall.

Would You Like a Topping
with That?

DO: Bond with family over frozen treats

DON'T: Treat family like a frozen bond

Chloe walked back up the meandering driveway and crossed paths with Stan, or what was a full-on view of Stan's crack, sadly exposed in bad Bermuda shorts. He was all bent out of shape cursing the Beemer's Assist computer system—you know, one of those things that, like, control a car's everything.

Stan kicked the door hard and lost a shearling moccasin in the process.

"Jesus, Chloe, good timing. Listen, you're good

with technical difficulties, no? Come here and show your old man somethin'."

Hmmm. He was talking to her like his usual, irritated, not-making-any-mention-of-her-disgracing-the-family self? A cell phone headset cord dangled from his ear, and a button popped off his current Hawaiian shirt—this one a poppy number with several ukuleles and totem poles going at it at once. Chloe eagerly went over to help.

"Sure thing, Dad. What's up?"

"What's up is this stupid mother—or, as Lupe would say, this pinche car—cost me eighty g's and I can't even set the goddamn clock! It's like NASA in there. That little, what do you call it, that mouse thing is so small I can't even see it let alone use the damn thing!" Stan patted the tiny beads of sweat on his forehead. Just like Zeyde.

"Dad, it can't be that hard. You just have to ask the car nicely and it'll do everything for you."

Stan did not look convinced.

"Maybe the car already knows the time? Like, has a satellite situation where you don't have to program anything."

"Oh yeah? I don't think so, Chlo."

He scooted on in the passenger side and pushed a series of buttons. A walnut panel lit up and a voice politely greeted them with "Good evening. Pardon me?"

"Just watch this," Stan whispered. "CLOCK ON!" he boomed.

"RADIO OFF," the car responded in a clipped, full-on-mechanized-but-kinda-English accent. Stan looked at Chlo like *See what I'm talking about?* Then he repeated "CLOCK! ON!"

"PARDON ME?" the car replied.

Stan gripped the wheel and repeated his request one more time.

"CLOCK ON!"

Nope. Not. On.

"CLOCK ON YOU GODDAMN PINCHE CAR! TELL ME THE GODDAMN TIME ALREADY!"

"CD CHANGER, THREE," the car replied.

Chloe didn't know what to do. The car was possessed.

"Oy gevalt!" Stan shook his head, cord dangling, one moccasin on, the other on the lawn, sad eyes looking at Chloe for kinda a while.

"Chloe doll, say . . . you wanna grab a yogurt?"

Shocked at the invitation, Chloe gushed, "Sure thing, Daddy!"

She prepared to switch seats with her dad but, to her surprise, he even let her drive. So she turned the ignition on and they headed down the driveway, into town, to the Promenade.

The Promenade food court was pretty standard mall fare but stepped up a couple notches—like, with sushi and chai. This, of course, was to service the finicky clientele who frequented the sprawling better-than-average shopping arcade. Seated in an upholstered booth, Chloe was trying her best not to style passersby and to keep her FD on the down low. But this was hard! Her mind was in overdrive as she sat next to her dad. Like, she hadn't been alone with him for months and she really wanted to say or do, or NOT say or do, whatever would make him forgive her.

"Don't you want one, Chlo?" he asked, rummaging through a deep pocket. Out popped a worn cocoa-colored wallet, water and coffee stains everywhere. Chloe leaned against the glass counter. Nope. No butterfat here. More like runny, watered-down lactose that was sure to unsatisfy but keep you coming back for more.

"Hmmm. I guess I'll have the same as you, Dad."

Stan rifled through a crumpled wad of bills while a young girl hopped up, her cheap plastic "FroYo Palace" visor coming into view. She was wearing an all-purpose "smocked" apron three sizes too big over an ankle-length skirt trailing to a pair of, like, white nurse shoes.

"Would you like a topping with that?" she chirped. Chloe stared blankly at the girl for a long time—no reply. The FroYo Palace gal politely grinned back, her grin becoming confused, uncomfortable, and then annoyed. . . .

Chloe blinked. "I'm sorry."

Stan and the FroYo Girl exchanged mutually confused looks.

"She asked you something, Chloe." He raised a furry brow.

"Oh, right. No thanks. No topping for me."

Chloe was still staring. Stan coughed. And then Chloe was unable to keep it to herself.

"That uniform just sucks!" she shouted. She had to. You know how when something didn't look right she just had to say something. "I mean, what I meant to say was: I'd really love to restyle your sucky uniform! Do you mind?"

Stan choked on a spoon while Chloe hopped over the counter. She grabbed a pad and pencil while both the girl and her dad stood stunned. And then Chlo started to draw, explaining what she was doing aloud.

"You see, the oversized smock and high-waisted A-line skirt do no justice to your silhouette. Doesn't this place realize that Calicuties like you are a, what would you call it, Dad? An asset. Yeah, cute girls in cute uniforms mean more customers with carbs to burn eating crappy, I mean, de-licious frozen yogurt! If only your manager would let me design something simple and fresh, something, like, cute, then you FroYo Palace gals would be la bomba at the Promenade. Really. No joke. I'll show you what I mean."

Chloe drew something cool and clean with tri-colored stripes—in part inspired by vintage Hot Dog on a Stick uniforms, minus the stupid hat. It was a look that, as the Countess would say, was *Swaucy Mary Quant Meets YSL Mondrian.* Chloe added smoky mod eyeliner and frosty lips, but frosty cool like the frozen yogurt—not frosty trailer park, like, bad mall victim. She drew white mid-calf go-go boots with exposed zippers, like her own, and offered to customize them herself. She even wrote down the number for the store in L.A. that carried the dead stock and felt very generous for sharing the valuable tip.

So in Mondrianish mini shifts cinched with logo-studded belts—a tiny band in milky white, orange, and blue that read "FroYo Palace" in the company's signature font, the change was a surefire way to make the place cool.

Chloe handed the manager a couple of napkins with the full-on sketched-out look. The girls were nodding in agreement, and the manager was thanking her no end. She hadn't meant to say or do anything. It all just kindaspontaneouslypouredout. Like, for some reason she felt inspired instead of afraid. She even felt really good for sharing, like she was being a model citizen of some kind. Then she realized her dad was sitting there too, listening. Like, listening for real. Stanley watched her in amazement while vanilla streaks ran down his chicken legs.

"You know, kiddo, I think you might be pretty good at this fashion business. But you oughta charge people for that kinda advice. You can't be giving it away for free! You may not bill four hundred an hour, but heck, every novice has to start out somewhere."

Chloe blushed as her dad patted her back, a definite sign of encouragement and, dare I say, forgiveness.

A Belt Is Never Just a Belt

DO: Top it off with a good accessory

DON'T: Be an accessory to stay on top

This had been an experiment, An Ode to Pleats and Ink, something Chloe thought she'd call the Look of Love.

The bodice of her strapless dress was severe and bone crushing but felt and fit right for the occasion. It was a silk and canvas bustier wrapped together by wide asymmetrical bands, kinda like a straightjacket. A long, lone red zipper twisted around one side and attached itself to a mini circle skirt of sorts: a thigh-skimming burst of black puffy lace, wool, and alternating plastic pleats, each the color of tarnished gold. At the last minute Chloe had felt compelled to smear it all with black ink with sponges and an old makeup brush. She had sewed the complicated piece herself for weeks while Pau nodded approvingly over dozens of telenovelas, Fritos, and Oreos.

A sudden cry, and Dante collapsed. *Ouch.* He quickly picked himself up off her dress and yawned. *Glad it was thrilling for you too.* Chloe watched him zip his gray peg-legged jeans and pull an olive sweater over his head. For the first time, Chloe noticed the red cuffs—a surprising detail.

Was that it? Were they done? She should've stayed home to watch telenovelas with Pau. Then again, Chloe felt like she had just cheated on Dante, but, like, in her head, with her clothes.

Her breath got really short and quick—she definitely felt like— You thought I was gonna say she was gonna cry, didn't you? No, au contraire, she felt pissed and ready to destroy. Or did she feel ready to create?

And then Dante fastened his belt: a studded, black and white checkered belt. Chloe winced. That was a girl's belt. Definitely a run-of-the-mill borderlinealternative belt that, like, could be purchased anywhere. She didn't own a belt like that. Who would've given him a belt? She had made him a customized, beautiful, one-of-a-kind belt and he didn't even wear it tonight. Her belt. Their belt. He, like, could've at least done that. Whose belt was this?

"I hate that belt," she muttered. That was about the best she could do. Or, like, say.

Dante shrugged.

"Oh yeah. It doesn't really matter, does it, Chlo? It's just a belt."

Just-a-belt. Well, that just-said-it-all.

Suddenly, Dante swelled up completely. He literally became an enormous, jumbo, red-flag-waving mayday-mayday—so saturated with red that any message inside was impossible to read!

That was it. She was dating a jumbo red flag who spoke a totally different language than her because if he, like, actually was sensitive *at all* and got who she *was* he would totally get that, like, a belt, was never just a belt!

Right about now Chloe felt like a cheap and used piece of non-vintage, secondhand shmatte. She wanted to see the Countess. Then she felt guilty, like she had just cheated on Dante not just with her clothes but also with the Countess. But wait; obviously Dante had been cheating on her with the Brazilian Shopgirl! Chloe felt confined and confused and wanted to take off the bone-crushing corset dress. Right. Now.

Chloe held her wristlet clutch close—a little zebra-print style, ruched at the sides, with a detachable bangle to loop over your wrist. She just got now why these things were called clutches.

"Dante," she ventured, "that belt doesn't even fit you. Or maybe it actually does. Or what I really meant to say, I guess, is . . . you don't really fit me."

Stunned, he blinked. She blinked too. Did she really just break up with him? Like, for real break up—break up with him?

"Whoa-whoa, hold up. Don't get all crazy here. It's just a friggin' belt. Sue has been talking trash—I knew it!"

"This has nothing to do with Sue."

"Then this is because of your family—"

"This has nothing to do with them either." Chloe sighed, since it wasn't really about any of them anymore.

"Then this is cuz my life isn't like yours, right? You know, the kind of life that makes it easier for you than me to get in?"

Get in where? This was, like, the most intense conversation she had ever had with Dante and the irony was that it would be their last. And yes, even though she could understand, she didn't agree.

"Dante, maybe getting in isn't so great. Like, once you're in you might not even like it! You might even realize you were only trying to *get* in cuz everyone around you told you how rad it would be when inside it totally blows. Or once you do get in, you, like, might not even bother to see what's really happening inside cuz, like, you were too focused on getting in rather than being there. Everyone's always talking about needing to get into this school or party or show or whatever. Once you're in, you might even be, like, Well, all right, now what? Is this even where I wanna be? Is this even who I am? Sometimes the answer's yes but it might also be no."

Whoa. That was kinda profound. Totally something the Countess would say. Even Pau. (Well, maybe not say it but she would definitely agree.) Chloe stood quite pleased at this little strand of pearls. Change was definitely in the air.

"Yo, what are you trippin' for now, Wong?"

"I'm saying that sometimes it takes time to know if you do or you don't. If you want in, or out."

Feeling resigned and kinda over it all, Chloe looked at Dante's long skinny scarf, his rugged goatee, his stupid Charger (well, all right, it was a pretty hot car). She finally saw him clearly. Sans flags and all. Sure Dante had always *looked* like a cool boyfriend. But he certainly didn't feel that way.

"Dante, I think I'll just walk home. Even though I'm really not wearing walking shoes."

Dante stood there stunned in his perfectly imperfect wardrobe, styled soo like-I-don't-even-care-but-maybe-now-that-Chloe-left-me-I-might cool.

"But I'll pick you up tomorrow after school, right?"

Chloe secured her thigh-skimming minidress and turned to go.

"No thanks, Dante. Besides, you always wanted a groupie more than a girlfriend."

SO . . . Chloe got out of *that* and was gonna start and finish something else—something positive once and for all. She felt a surge of simultaneous panic and inspiration. She *FINALLY* was gonna mail her Saint Martins app FOR REAL.

portfolio

To whom it may concern,

I know, I know. You already know she applied, duh, you're reading this. But you might want to know what happened *next*.

After the whole mailing the Saint Martins app thing was said and done . . . it was like this.

To Prom or Not to Prom

DO: Experiment with mixed-media materials

DON'T: Mix with materialistic media

Chloe's complete portfolio was currently under review at Saint Martins admissions in London. She had grouped together what was her very first, pretend, real collection. Would her Ode to Cali theme be well received way out in the UK? Chloe was shvitzing all over just thinking about it.

West Coast WASP *did* turn out fab-tastic, a neat ensemble she designed with Spring in mind; all bubblegum pink and herringbone tweed. Then there was

Punk-Rock Chola for Sue, an easy transitional school-to-bar look combining chola-femme trims but with punk-rock hardware. Velour Relief was an eclectic tribute to Pau and Zeyde, a departure from the world of wovens for finicky, harder-to-handle knits. And her Swashbuckling Siren would wear a silk taffeta extravaganza befitting any bombshell, operagoer, circus performer, or risqué contessa. Then there was this, the final look, her pièce de résistance, but would it ever be featured?

Chloe pondered the possibility while she and Sue were glued to the terrace . . . kinda like Lucinda but not. They couldn't stop gawking at all the activity going on across the street. Enormous boxes had been coming and going for weeks and there hadn't been a summons from the Countess forever! Where was Julius? Was the Countess moving? Was she, ohgodno, dead?

Chloe was too afraid to ring the bell and say hello—she would never pop on over SANS invite. So she resolved to write the Countess a little thank-you note instead, deep inside the closet.

So you know by now Chlo's closet was, like, her sanctuary. Even though he would never admit it aloud, Stan knew this too. For Chloe's sweet sixteen Stanley even commissioned some rad architect to totally revamp the space. He designed three tiny keyhole windows that looked out into the garden, an expansive range of purple mountains fanning wide in the distance. Airy and bright with impossibly high cathedral ceilings, the creamy gardenia space was a sacred temple only Chloe was ever allowed to enter to pray—I mean arrange.

No matter how down and out Chloe felt, cataloging her closet always gave her, like, hope. Color-coding sweaters, scarves, and skirts brought about clarity, even inner peace. Adding little heart stickers or notes to an accessory's accompanying Polaroid provided intense relief. It was like meditation. Or medication. Or was it just serotonin again?

Chloe sat down to hand-sew her signature at the bottom of her little thank-you note. She sealed it with a fancy-pants wax seal, the kind the Countess would just adore.

Dear Countess,

A little note to say thank you for changing my life. I don't know yet if I got into Saint Martins, but, like, your letter of rec still meant so much. Are you going away? I hope there is time to see you before you leave. I would like to show you what I am making for prom—even though I'm not going.

Sincerely with love,
Chloe

So Chloe was definitely not going to attend prom. After all, she clearly did NOT have a date. She wouldn't be the right date for Peter over at EP either. He deserved to go with someone cool who wanted to go for real, not pretend.

"I don't get why we just don't go to that club of your folks' to lie out. There's a bigger pool there. And a bar." Sue was now sprawled out on the balcony working on her already perfect tan.

"Sue-Lou, is that all you can think about? Besides, you'd get us kicked out for indecent exposure."

"Very funny, Wong, and hello, you were the one who crocheted this halter for me! And what's more important right now is this: Are you feeling prom or not?"

Chloe didn't want to think about prom. She was enjoying refolding cream cardigans. It was like planting flowers in a garden but not.

"C'mon, Chlo, it's one night of the rest of your life. Plus I make a much hotter date than Dante any day!"

Chloe laughed. "Sue-Lou, relax, I already said I'd make your dress."

"Wong, this isn't about the dress! It's about showing up, like, to represent."

Sue hopped up, all serious.

"Que what?" Chloe laughed. "I don't feel all too representative of Roosevelt, Sue."

"Not Roosevelt, girl. *You,* you fool!"

She threw her hands up and rolled over on her back.

Oh. Chloe hadn't thought about it like that.

A Bow Tie Is Never
Just a Bow Tie

DO: Admit when you need help fixing your tie

DON'T: Assume ties can be fixed overnight

Chloe felt like she was getting some kind of postgrad thing together. There was nothing left to lose and nothing more to hide. She had gotten off academic probation (barely) and even reluctantly confessed to her dad about the whole applying to Saint Martins scenario and how even if she didn't get in or they wouldn't let her go she still felt better and transformed for finally finishing something for once. Stan wasn't exactly bouncing up and down at this information (can you imagine?) but he did listen to her without taking a single incoming call—a huge improvement.

And apparently Stan had been doing some homework of his own about Saint Martins—shocked to have learned from a revered and trusted client that Saint Martins was an A-list kind of place.

So Stan had a change of heart—sort of. If things didn't work out he said he'd put in some calls to a big client in "shmatte" and try to hook her up with a summer internship at a "tried-and-true Newport design firm." Chloe didn't want to ask for favors but she felt relieved that her dad was on her side for once. He even promised her that together they'd "figure out a plan."

They discussed these "plans" over frozen yogurt. And, to her total pink surprise, the girls over at FroYo Palace took all her stylin' cues and transformed their uniforms to a tee. It was CarboLite FroYo on the house and much-needed points with Stan for Chlo! Chloe couldn't help but blush when they came over to thank her, a gesture that I think made Stan burst right outta his Hawaiian shirt with pride! Oh, and Chloe told Stan that she and Dante were *done,* which of course made him have to spontaneously go to the bathroom while also making, like, his year.

But what about Lucinda? It might take a while before she could admit that her firstborn wasn't going to a college on the Wong-Leiberman list but at least she wouldn't gripe about it if the Bacon Bringer was on Chlo's side. Oh, but wait, that's right, Lucinda hadn't really been home. She had left on a month-long Ikebana tour of Japan. Kinda like rehab.

Would this discovery trip be critical to Lucinda's evolution and, dare I say, survival? To all the Wong-Leibermans' survival? Because if Chloe didn't get in to Saint Martins they would all still be living under the same ten-thousand-square-foot roof.

Oy vey ew.

Oh, all right. Half-oy-vey-ew. Life just might be acceptable. Not ideal, but acceptable. And then there was a tiny knock on her door.

Mitchell?

"To what do I owe this pleasure?" Chlo asked, fully engrossed in collage. She was making a new collage of Polaroids and didn't really want any distractions of the Young Republican kind.

"I need your help, Chlo." Mitchell walked into her room hesitantly, treading really really light. His baby pink oxford was untucked and open at the neck, three buttons undone, chest exposed—all out of character. Chloe was confused by such an unusual, ungroomed sight. In his hands he cradled a sorry-looking bow tie. It was a crumpled, severed mess.

"My bow tie. It—I don't know how it broke. Do you think you could fix it?"

Chlo's eyes bulged, a la Zeyde.

"As ifffff, traitor!"

"Hey, Chloe, can we like, try to keep the peace? You might be living here, uh, unexpectedly and I'd like to feel like I'm not in a war zone. Besides, diplomacy is the new way to shock and awe."

"Give me one good reason why I should be nice to you!"

Mitchell dug his hands deep inside his khaki pockets.

"I'm waiting—"

Mitchell kicked the shag rug and looked away.

"Spit it out, Mitch—like, please."

Mitchell swallowed hard. And then he blurted the unthinkable.

"Gypsy."

Gao-chaw?

"That's low, Mitch. Real low."

He hadn't brought that up, like, since, forever. . . .

"But it's true. Gypsy is a good reason."

Mitch looked uncharacteristically shy, small even.

"I don't get it, Mitch. I don't get you either."

"Look, Chloe. You and I might think like different breeds. You are, however, still my sister which means we are related (although sometimes I don't know how), and so, if nothing else, we share significant . . . history. I still remember how it used to be. And for some reason, that very first time you showed me how to wear a bow tie, well, clearly I can't seem to forget it."

"But it wasn't, like, for real, Mitch!"

Chloe couldn't believe the conversations she was having lately.

"But you liked the way it looked."

Was he kidding?

"But, Mitchell, it wasn't like, supposed to be interpreted literally."

"Well, I'm a literal kind of guy!"

Chlo paused to consider this valid point. But, like, what was his point?

"You're telling me that, for real, you remember the time I showed you how to tie a bow tie and that it affected you?"

Mitch shifted in his Top-Siders. Yep, still sans socks.

"I remember everything, Chloe. Kinda like you but—like me."

Then why did he pretend not to remember at all? Should she try to forgive and if not forget then move on? Or, like, take this talking-about-things-aloud thing in stages?

"Give me your stupid bow tie."

Chloe assessed the damage close. Definite repairs were in order. No immediate turnaround here. The fabric was ripped and not just at the seams.

"Mitchell, if I do this for you can you at least, well, like, could you be open to mixing it up sometimes, maybe an untucked as opposed to a tucked button-down? You know, keep it a bit imperfect—try to make it, like, ironic?"

Mitchell looked confused.

"Never mind."

"Well then, Chloe, I guess I'll check the status after prom. You are going to prom, right?"

Gao-chaw?

"C'mon, Chlo—the people need something new to talk about."

Huh. This was true.

"I do have a fabtastic dress, or suit, rather."

"I'm sure you do." Mitchell looked Chloe straight in the eye, resolved to, like, drop some kind of bomb.

"Chloe," he ventured, "this might be hard for you

to believe but I went into Brooks Brothers that day thinking of you. I thought you'd think the bow-tie decision was different. Alternative. Maybe even cool."

"How could you think that?" Chloe blurted. "You assumed because I dressed you up in a bow tie when you were seven that I thought it would look good for real?"

"I thought it would make me more mature. I guess you could say I got attached more than anything—to the bow tie—to what it reminded me of—oh, whatever, Chlo. It wasn't about the way it looked, all right—it was about the way it made me feel. You of all people can understand that. Right?"

Was he, like, trying to relate or apologize or something?

This was complicated.

"Hey, Gypsy," Chloe sighed, "instead of making assumptions why don't you just ask me what I mean. I'll even try to do the same. And, like, I'm sorry for dissing your bow tie way back when."

Mitch nodded, extending his hand. They shook firmly. It was a bit tricky, but it was a start.

Represent

D✪: Try new people and places

D✪N'T: Let new people and places try you

"**TRL**—Totally Roosevelt Live!" Read the Cheez-Whiz banner strung high across the thirty-sixth-floor ballroom of the El Conejo Hyatt. Energetic. Exuberant. Exposed. All the things a high school prom banner should be. Sue and Chloe rolled in last minute, holding hands and checking out the scene.

"Promise we'll only stay, like, ten minutes max?" Chloe begged. This was, after all, so embarrassing.

"It's prom, girl! And yes it's lame but we paid. We're

here. We look fabulous—it's a testament to our survival. We made it through high school!" Sue seemed more convinced that chillin' for the night at the El Conejo Hyatt might actually be a good time. In a plum bikini top and a voluminous ballgown skirt, black Chucks poking out, Sue looked just like a chola princess, a hottie-tottie, but polished, for sure. It was an Ode to Sugar and Spice, the decided-upon theme for her night.

The only reason Chloe came at all was to feature her last look, period. She decided that this final high school look would be her true pièce de résistance. Dante didn't deserve to be credited with that.

Her Last Look merged, by far, the most complex elements Chloe had incorporated yet.

These were her notes for inspiration:

PROM IS:
Open
Closed
Punk Rock
Contessa
YSL (smoking or not?)
Hat or Hibiscus?
Buttercups—yellow, not peanut butter
Buttahcreammmmmm
Opaque bands
Lace inserts
Crystals? Sour lemon ones
Satin ties NOT bows
Leg-o'-mutton slash angel-wing sleeves

Fur slash feather sacrifice

EdwardianVictorian

Rock and roll

Ballerinas

Gold dust

Fantasy

Fritos

SUE-LOU IS:

Bikini

Beads

PLUM

Clouds

Ballrooms

Ruffles

Chuck Ts

Rubies

POLISHED PUNK ROCK

Chloe had spent hours poring over old photos and books getting inspired. She had firmly decided on a suit rather than a dress and wanted to merge several fabrics and eras together as one.

She was in lovelovelove with this white YSL tuxedo-y getup Bianca Jagger made famous decades back when she wed Mick (an event the Countess had recounted fondly even though she insisted that, contrary to popular belief, La Bianca did not wear pants). Chloe wanted to reinterpret her wedding look now— the feelings of celebration and commitment, not the literal look. She also was in love with leg-o'-mutton sleeves, these crazy drumstick-looking things made popular in Edwardian England. Or was it Victorian? Huh. Well, she wanted to do something like that too. And then of course she had to be tough, so there had to be something punk rock thrown in the mix. In the end, she pulled off all three.

Chloe created a suit that was white but in varying shades. Accessories and embellishments were yellow with the tiniest hints of red and gold. She definitely didn't want to wear a gigantic hat like Bianca so she settled on a crystal, yes crystal, diadem, "a little gifty" also from the Countess (who apparently had been gifted lots of crystal-y gifts . . .).

Chlo's jacket was kinda Victorian—a high collar that fastened with delicate crystal (yes, crystal) buttons the color of lemonade. The structured bodice had a fitted peplum with tiny piping in soft buttercream and tiny snippets of lace. The sleeves were, like, a hybrid. Leg-o'-muttonish and like angel wings. (I say leg-o'-muttonish because the shoulders were like big embellished, furry, feathered mutton-sticks but angel-like too because they wrapped around and attached like wings.) The detachable sleeves could snap off at the elbows, like, if she got hot in all those feathers and fur. They snapped onto ribbed cotton cuffs at the elbows—really long ones that grazed the knuckles and wrapped into the fingers, like punk-rock fingerless gloves. Or cuffs. Glovecuffs.

Her pants were fitted knickers, also shown in ivory

silk wool. Yellow lace inserts were sewn along the seams—little floral webs that exposed the tiniest bit of skin, running the length of the hips. The fabric gathered at the knees with a buttery ribbed cotton band, yellow silk lining sewn underneath it all.

Chloe's ruby round-toe shoes balanced on slivers of real gold heels (also courtesy of La Contessa), long ruby and gold satin ties lacing around her calves like a schizophrenic ballerina goddess.

Before leaving 450 Avocado Lane, Chloe untied her yellow corsage (something her dad handed her through tears and Pau attached through juk) to add the single yellow hibiscus behind her left ear, ditching the tiara. Overall, the look was serious but romantic, open and closed, soft like the fur and hopeful like the wings.

It was an ode to three different eras, something way old, something in-between, and something still au courant.

That was it! She would call her last look an Ode to Three—or maybe even an Ode to FD?

Last Looks

DO: Look for love in unexpected places

DON'T: Expect love to keep you in one place

Well, showing up to prom did signal a change of something inside, a turning point, a decision made at a crossroad of life. The Last Look was really more of a New Beginning! The *End* of an Era for real! High school be gone! Chloe felt light as a feather and giddy with anticipation. And giddy with hunger, too. She had skipped dinner to finish styling Sue and needed Fritos, bad. The lime-colored sign of the patron saint of late-night eaters, 7-Eleven, glowed in the distance. Thank gawd.

Chloe stood in line with a supersized bag of Fritos and some jalapeno sauce when she definitely felt someone watching her. Peter? No.

It was a very chicy-chic lady. She was old. She must have been, like, at least thirty, but pretty hot. She was wearing an impeccably sleek duster coat, the deep V contrasting well with her impossibly high-knotted ponytail. Her nails were crimson, short and square, fingers done up with an impressive set of right-hand rocks featured only on her middle fingers. A chunky red bracelet was the only splash of color on her otherwise black palette. She was definitely rad, in an uptown-downtown kind of way. What was she doing at a 7-Eleven in El Conejo?

Chloe nodded coolly with her half-opened bag of chips and left. The woman followed her in total Manhattan stride.

"Excuse me," she said. Chloe stopped. She couldn't imagine what the woman could want but she was getting pretty used to spontaneous encounters with all kinds.

"Whoooo made your suit?" she asked.

"Um, no one you'd know." Mouth full of Fritos, Chloe blushed and turned to walk away.

The woman clickety-clacked after her at an accelerated pace.

"But you must tell me! It's absolutely dandy but not! So soft and sleek, tough yet supple—full of whimsy and charm."

This woman was a walking, talking . . . Chloe

couldn't bring herself to use the F word (you know which played-out word I'm talking about), but that *was* exactly what she *was*. Chloe couldn't help but smile.

"Want a Frito?" Chloe offered. She held the bag out, feeling totally retarded.

"Oooooh, I haven't had one of these for years." The woman dipped a finger in the bag and nibbled a single chip.

"Thank you. But you didn't sayyy, whoooo are you featuring?"

Chloe's eyes lit up. The woman had just used, like, her favorite verb, EVER!

"Oh, I guess, me?"

The woman's eyes lit up too.

"Reee-ally. So you're a designer then."

"Not exactly," Chloe whispered.

"A stylist?"

"Nooo . . ."

"Shy and elusive one, hum? Come and tell me, who's your rep?"

"I'm . . . in between reps, right now?"

"Then where can I see your line? Are you based in N.Y. or L.A.?"

"Um . . . neither."

"Good, then you're below the radar. But tell me! Whooo carries your line?"

Carries her line. Was she for real?

"Well, I'm not exactly in stores."

"Even better. So you do custom pieces, one-offs, or just ready-to-wear?"

"Sometimes all three," Chloe blurted.

A town car slowly appeared, purring alongside the curb.

"Look, sweetie, I'm sooo terribly late for my flight." The lady unclutched her Birkin bag, a real one, and unfolded a metallic case that held a set of tiny cards. "Cahhll me Monday. We'll figure out a plan."

Intrigued, the mystery woman slipped into the car, one stiletto at a time.

"Unreal. There just might be hope this season yet! And to think, way out west on the coast."

The town car proceeded to drive away, and then abruptly stopped. A window zipped down and the chicy-chic lady raised a hand to her angular chin, calling after Chloe one last time . . .

"Yoo-hoo! Designer girl! But I didn't get your name?"

Chloe looked at the card in dismay and then at the woman—now suspended in a way-pink cloud, pinker than any cloud she'd seen, like, EVER!

"Chloe Leiberman—s-sometimes Wong!" she stammered, not quite believing her kind of luck.

The woman nodded approvingly; she even, dare I say, smiled.

"That's just a fabulous name," the Manhattan lady purred, winking and waving goodbye as the town car faded into the warm, ohsoCali night.

And that was how it was.

THE END.

[But you know the end is always just the beginning, don't you? Of course you do. . . .]

Chloe Glossary

YIDDISH: rhymes with kiddish. The unofficial language of MOTs, members of the tribe, as in the tribes of Israel.

NOSH: rhymes with mosh. To snack.

SANS: rhymes with Cons, as in the sneakers. Means without, as in without a postgrad plan.

OV VEY: rhymes with boy-day. An exaggerated sigh of lament.

FAUX PAS: faux pronounced fo, like fo real; pas pronounced pau, like Chlo's Chinese gram. Means a big ol' DON'T.

HI-YAAA: hmm . . . this one can be used in several ways to express irritation or aggravation, and is always screamed, never said, just like Jackie Chan would say when kicking someone hard. Often accompanied by an eye roll, snort, or slap, the yaaaa should be accentuated to show the extent of your how-could-you-be-so lame, dumb, etc., feeling. . . .

KOK NAY GAN TUH!: pronounced as spelled. An expression as if to say, You are so stupid I feel compelled to smack you in the head.

OY GEVALT!: like fry the salt. Means oh jeez this is terrible. . . .

KOSHER: rhymes with oh sure! Literally means fit to eat but also means it's all good, which this information most certainly was not.

COUTURE: rhymes with too pure. Means high, high fashion.

LO-FAN: Cantonese for white people. This is not to be confused with lo-fun, which means flat white noodles (when stir-fried in tomato-flavored beef, a particularly tasty dish Pau likes).

TAT-TAT-HIGH: tat-tat like hot hot. Backless slippers favored by old Chinese ladies so it's easier to rub Tiger Balm onto their unfortunately cracked heels.

BALENCIAGA: the great Basque master of dress and illusion—a leader of Spanish couture, definitely NOT what Lucinda was wearing.

EURO-METROSEXUAL: OK, so unless you've been in a coma the past four years you already know that a metrosexual is not a gay guy (but could be) but is someone with a good sense of style who moisturizes, maybe owns a product or two. So add the Euro and imagine Euro-styling details like turned-up collars and sockless loafers. . . .

PLOTZ: rhymes with lots. Means to burst or explode, which can be either a good or bad thing depending on the situation.

CHOZZERAI: said all Bob-Fosse-jazz-hands style. Literally means pork, but really means crap. (Strangely enough, in Cantonese the word for pork, "char-su," is pronounced quite similarly to the Yiddish "chozzerai.")

L'CHAYIM: rhymes with OH BUY THEM! Means TO LIFE! and is said like you're hawking a loogie: "Luuuk-HI-AM!"

FI-DI-LA: rhymes with why-see-ma? Means wrap it up already.

LUFTMENSH: rhymes with fluffed bench. Means exactly what Zeyde said.

GUNG HAY FAT CHOY: means Happy New Year. Gung like Jung, as in Karl JUNG and hay like day, fat like bought, and choy with boy or toy or both.

SHLEMIEL: pronounced shla-meal. An idiot, a numbskull, a fool.

MESHUGGE: pronounced mu like mushy; shug like Suge Knight, the formerly incarcerated rapper; uh like duh. MU-SHUG-GUH means CRA-ZY.

CHUTZPA: the gall, the nerve, also the balls, even guts. Is hurled, not said, and loud. Chut like foot, zpah like spa.

SHMATTE: rhymes with gotta. A cheap and shoddy rag, useless dreck, something not kosher to wear.

SHVITZING: shh-vitz-ing. To sweat like a beast (do beasts even sweat?).

FAI-JI: like pay-day. Means fat boy in Cantonese.

BOK-GUI: rhymes with bok choy, the leafy green vegetable, but means white ghost.

MO LAY YEL: no way sisters. Pronounced as sounds, and loud.

PALAZZO PAJAMAS: once upon a time when terry cloth Juicys and velour JLos did not yet exist, ladies lounged for the evening in these sassy, silky wide-legged numbers.

ROGER VIVIER: Rooojer Viviyeah! A master, a visionary, a great Parisian shoe designer who even made shoes for the queen.

CHIN-SEN-PAU: means crazy lady, which Pau kinda is but, like, in a good way.

TIT DA JOW: rhymes with bit a cow. Aforementioned Tiger Balm.

GAO-CHAW: rhymes with ow-straw. Means you've-got-to-be-kidding-me and yes, it's like the only thing Chlo knows how to say in Cantonese, except for Happy New Year.

MO-YUNG: mo like oh, yung like jung, again, as in Karl Jung. Means totally useless.

CHOLA: rhymes with cola. Spanish slang for a girl who looks tough and might be very capable of kicking your ass.

SANTERA: a high priestess of the Santeria faith and no, they're not crazy people who kill chickens for fun!

KIBBITZ: to shmooze, to socialize—kib as spelled, bitz like fits.

MUSLIN: cheapy fabric to practice sewing with, just in case you mess up, which is highly encouraged, the messing-up part that is.

FAT-MUNG: fat like bought. Mung like jung, again, as in Karl Jung. To be absentminded, distracted; to daydream excessively.

PINCHE: Spanish slang that rhymes with finchy. Means damn! but as an adjective—worthless, stupid, and usually annoying.

SUR-JEN: pronounced as spelled. Means insolent girl.

PEIGNOIR: pronounced pen-waaa. A little floaty nightie number, usually a see-through one.

HABERDASHERY: pertains to everything tailor-made, traditionally for men.

DEAD STOCK: retail goods left over from way back in the day so, like, they're prime unused vintage.

SAUTOIR: rhymes with po-twa. A drapey bracelet.

CLARO QUE SI: rhymes with borrow-a-T. Means but of course, en español. Sometimes just "claro" is used.

GAUCHOS: rhymes with Grouchos. Really wide culottes—shaped like floods but shorter, to the knee.

CAFTAN: like a muu-muu, but a chic one, to the floor, like Rosy would wear—think Istanbul and exotic ladies on great big terraces overlooking sand and sea.

CREEPERS: an og punk-rock shoe, on the Herman Munster tip—and actually like a wingtip, except on an elevated, platform sole.

LA FAMILIA ES TODO: family is everything, blood is everything, "es todo."

SHLEP: means to go the distance with difficulty. Schl like shhl. Ep like yep. Shha-lep.

SMOCKED: made by gathering fabric in little bunched-up stitches, like, on decorative maid's aprons or Heidi-ish folk-dancer garb.

LOW-MEAN PAU: means mean and bitter old lady, just like Chloe said.

JUK: rhymes with book. Chinese porridge with assorted gross stuff in it. Probably not kosher.

MO-DOM: like no gum. Means got no guts.

PINTUCKS: tiny raised seams kinda like pleats. Decorative and functional, very cool.

PUTA: Am I allowed to say what this means? For real, it's not very nice.

TOUCHÉ: too-shay. Means you got me, like, you're right.

CHUTZPA: again, pronounced like you're hawking a loogie: Hootzpah (like foot-spa). Means, like, the nerve.

SHMENDRICK: pronounced as spelled. A hopeless, desperate, wimpy dork.

SHLUB: Like tub. A shlub looks like the word sounds, all bloblike.

EMBELLISHMENT: the "fancy" way to refer to the bells and whistles sewn onto a garment, also known as TRIM.

MAVEN: an expert, which, on the topic of style, Spring was certainly not.

SCHMALTZ: rhymes with waltz. Literally means chicken fat but I'm sure you get the point.

SHMOOZ: to mingle, to hobknob, to mix for the cause, usually a selfish one.

NEBBISH: kinda a loser, but a sweet one who you feel bad for cuz he means well, which brings me to mensh. . . .

MENSH: rhymes with bench. An absolute cutie-pie, someone you want to mush up into a little ball because he is that sweet.

TÊTE-À-TÊTE: rhymes with get-ah-pet. Means a little get-together.

HAUTE COUTURE: pronounced oat like oatmeal, cootour. Means the best of the best, la crème de la crème, in design, not ice cream.

PIÈCE DE RÉSISTANCE: pee-es-doo-ray-zees-tahns! The final destination, the end of the road, the culmination of greatness.

PEPLUM: ruffly detail sewn at the waist. Usually on a jacket but can be on a dress.

AU COURANT: rhymes with oh, mo-ron. Means in-the-know and now.

Carrie Rosten is a Chinese/Polish/Jewish WASP who did go to college. A graduate of UCLA, she has designed and owned her own women's clothing line; sold designs to costume designers for *Friends* and *The OC;* and been a stylist for rap videos, pop-punk bands, supermodels, party girls, airline commercials, and indie films. She has also been a creative consultant for Mattel, American Girl, Loews Hotels, and Hard Candy cosmetics.

Writing runs in her quirky family. Her grandfather Leo Rosten wrote dozens of screenplays and books, including *The Joys of Yiddish;* her great-uncle William Steig wrote many children's books, including *Shrek.* In her spare time, the bicoastal author eats sushi, reads trashy magazines, and compulsively shops while drinking soy chai lattes.